GALAXY MOTEL

GALAXY MOTEL

MARK FURNESS

Liquorice Light Publishing

Mark Furness is a bestselling writer of thrillers and dark comedy crime.

A former journalist and foreign correspondent in the US, the UK, Australia, and East Asia, Mark's stories often feature reporters, a prime example being the international conspiracy thriller, *Under Eden.*

Mark is Australian and based in Sydney.

Learn more at: www.markfurnesswriter.com

Galaxy Motel is Book 3 in the *Firefly Electrics Series* of dark comedy crime thrillers featuring electricians Lennie and Joe, and their cockatoo, Rawcus.

Firefly Electrics Series:

#1 Justice Machine

#2 Kangaroo Court

#3 Galaxy Motel

About Galaxy Motel:

Lennie, Joe, and Rawcus are haunted by underworld rumours that have linked them to a fortune in cash, belonging to terrorists, that fell onto a city wharf during a cargo-loading accident.

When visitors carrying unusual tools, and wearing hardhats and sunglasses, knock on their front door, the trio needs to dance fast to avoid losing life or limb. They enlist the help of a blow-up doll named Mavis, a homemade electric chair, and the Galaxy Motel.

Meanwhile, their childhood friend, Pauline Gerrity, needs assistance to deal with a professional man who has a keen eye for underage girls who reside at Pauline's refuge for abused mothers and their children. They've dubbed the man Mr Teflon for good reason: he's a police force insider with a degree in psychology. Could a fantastic trip to a beach house help to rewire Mr T's soul and make the world safer?

One thing's for sure, Lennie, Joe, and Rawcus keep learning that the best-laid plans of cockatoos and men often go awry. Lennie is planning a seance to give the Scottish poet Robbie Burns an update on his fabled mice angle...

*The Firefly Electrics books are written in UK/Australian English.

1 - ALIENS

THE THREE figures squeezed onto the front porch of Lennie's terrace house didn't look like the last of the Enoka brothers, or the men of Middle Eastern appearance he'd been expecting to arrive, unannounced at any time of the day or night, but most probably in the dark.

Sitting at his kitchen table, Lennie studied live video of the visitors on his laptop screen, captured by a mini-cam hidden inside a spider's web that he'd spun into an upper corner of the porch using a spray can from a party shop.

The trio's lemon-fluoro safety vests were playing havoc with his equipment's colour-scales, but the matching hardhats perched atop their skulls displayed a clear corporate logo: *Sydney Water*.

Lennie sensed the motley trio knew as much about industrial-scale plumbing as his neighbour's one-eyed black cat, Bruce, who was deboning a rat on the step outside the open door from Lennie's kitchen to the back garden.

The biggest hard-hatter rapped his knuckles on the front door. One of his colleagues, who was almost as skinny as the long-handled shovel he was carrying, shuffled behind him.

The third, rounder visitor, held a red, arm's-length tube which Lennie figured might contain a rolled-up map about water pipes – or it might contain a venomous snake, a squeeze-shooter of sulphuric acid, a cyanide-salted baguette sandwich, a Molotov cocktail in a slender bottle...the list went on in Lennie's mind, which was juggling the molecules of a joint of Mars Grass he'd smoked minutes earlier.

The biggest hardhat was carrying an official-looking black satchel tucked under an arm from which even more possibilities radiated.

"Piss off," Lennie groaned aloud to his thoughts, which he could see breeding inside his brain faster than summer flies on outback roadkill.

"That won't get rid of them," said Joe.

Standing beside a kitchen bench, Joe towel-dried a floral-patterned china teapot. He was careful with the Queen of England's Silver Jubilee commemorative tea set, which was an heirloom handed down by Lennie's dead Aunty Doreen. He glanced at Lennie's laptop screen.

"Do you reckon it's them?"

Lennie rubbed his chin. "There's a quick way to find out."

High in a corner of the kitchen, a sulphur-crested cockatoo was riding a broomstick with an old-fashioned straw head that was secured by two ropes to ceiling hooks.

"Find out!" the bird screeched, rolling upside down on the stick before swinging by one claw with Olympian aplomb.

"That's what I like about you, Rawcus," Lennie replied, blinking at a flickering perception that the bird was a very small person wearing a white-feathered Mardi Gras costume. "Original thinking."

"You can talk! You fool!" Rawcus shot back, returning to the top of the broomstick in a blur of flapping wings.

Watching Rawcus astride the stick reminded Joe of the witch in a storybook he'd been given for his adult literacy class homework and that he had read yesterday to some kids at his friend Pauline Gerrity's refuge for women and children.

Lennie shut his laptop lid and winked at Joe. "They don't look like tea drinkers to me. Special brew?"

Joe nodded and opened a cupboard. "Just give me a sec."

Thunk! Thunk! Thunk!

"Mate," Lennie said. "I think if we don't Open Sesame pronto, we'll have a terrible mess on our hands that'll be visible from the street."

Joe shared Lennie's concern about the possible creation of a police-magnet if the door got busted and hell broke loose. Best to get these visitors inside. He spooned his home-blend coffee mix into a glass plunger pot and whistled a happy tune from Disney's *Snow White*. He used tongs to place white cubes from a jar into a sugar bowl. Joe patted his pink and blue, hibiscus-print apron. "Ready."

Lennie went to the kitchen sink and splashed cold water on his face, deliberately leaving a few tell-tale droplets on his freshly shaven skull. He stepped from the kitchen into the sitting room where he glanced in a wall mirror and hand-brushed his tight black T-shirt and skinny jeans before hoofing barefoot along the hallway to the door. He opened it and grinned wet-browed at the visitors. "Sorry, I was in the shower. Can I help you?"

The chunky leader was wearing wraparound sunglasses; a blue teardrop was tattooed under one of his eye sockets. He said, "We're from *Sydney Water*, sir. I'm afraid there's a blockage in the sewers that run through the back of this group of houses. We need to investigate."

"Now?" said Lennie, trying to disguise his dislike of people who faked tears.

"Yes, sir. There are several houses downhill from you where the toilets are blocked and overflowing. If yours are not already, you will be next."

"Shit," said Lennie.

Mr Teardrop grunted and impatiently switched his satchel from hand to hand.

This was a humourless character on a humourless mission, concluded Lennie. But what was the mission? "So you'd like to take your team through to our back garden, and do some digging by the look of it?"

"If it's not inconvenient."

Lennie tried to fathom hardhat's accent. It didn't sound foreign or have a Middle Eastern flavour. It was more Aussie-outback, Pommy-heritage, white farm-boy. Maybe they really were from *Sydney Water*. "Come in."

As the leader stepped to the same foot-level with Lennie inside the doorway, Lennie looked up and noted that this bloke was as big as Joe, which was pretty big, so he would be hard to put down if hand-to-hand combat erupted. Lennie reminded himself where his brass knuckleduster was located.

The sun-burned shovel-carrier was about Lennie's height and wiry. The words *love* and *hope* were tattooed under his major knuckles. He had the poise of a stick-fighter from the Billy Tang Martial Arts Academy up the street. Lennie gave himself a better than even chance there.

The tube carrier's body looked remarkably like a basketball that had four, raw beef sausages plugged into it. The appendages were trying to pass themselves off as arms and legs. Lennie conceded that the strange limbs, and the likeness of her head to a sweet potato, were probably exacerbated by the Mars Grass. There was a faint line of dark fuzz on the skin above her red-lipsticked top lip, which was part of a quite voluptuous pair, Lennie had to acknowledge, edible even, like two boiled cocktail franks squeezed together. He felt hungry and fought the urge to take a bite.

The visitors kept their sunglasses and hardhats on as they politely brushed their boots on the doormat, and stepped inside. Lennie closed the door behind them, feeling uneasy about the fact these plumbers wanted to protect their skulls *inside* the house. And their work boots were far too clean. It was as if these characters were so confident, or stupid, or disrespectful of their targets, that they couldn't be bothered applying some mud as a disguise. That sort of stuff was Camouflage 101, for fuck's sake.

"Ah," Lennie silently told himself, "don't be paranoid, maybe they're just spick and span types."

"Gidday," said Joe. The tangled mop of his red hair brushed the top of the door arch as he stepped from the kitchen into the sitting room to greet his guests. With five people inside it, the living space felt as crowded as a peak hour bus and smelled like pea and ham soup. Joe noticed sweat dripping from the biggest hardhat's brow, and it was a cool day, so he shot a wink at Lennie.

"The garden's out there through the kitchen," said Lennie, waving a hand into the adjoining room like a wanky waiter directing customers to a table. "Just step around the cat. He's blind in one eye and as deaf as a doornail, so there's no point trying to talk to him."

The visitors shuffled into the kitchen – skinny carrying his shovel; ball-girl her long red tube; and big hardhat his shifty leather satchel.

"Giss a kiss, love!" demanded Rawcus, rocking on his broomstick before tumbling over to swing by one claw and poke out his pink tongue.

Big hardhat and his female sidekick ducked from the shock of threatened sexual assault and turned towards the source. The shovel carrier was slow off the mark, as if he was hard of hearing, eventually following his companion's gazes and poking the shovel at Rawcus like a medieval lance.

"Easy, mate," Joe growled at the shovel man. "You're not that good looking."

With Lennie and Joe in the living room and the front door shut, and with all three hardhats in the kitchen, the biggest hardhat reached into his satchel – and whipped out a pistol.

He pointed the gun in the direction of Lennie and Joe, swinging its nose from man-to-man.

"Alright, cunts," he growled. "Let's stop fucking around. We want the money. Now!"

Lennie and Joe sighed and looked at each other like joggers after a marathon who thought they'd finished only to be told there was more to go.

"What money?" said Lennie, wondering if these visitors knew what was under the floor in their garden shed.

"Don't fuck with me, son." Big hardhat aimed at Lennie's chest. "We know all about the wharf."

*

About a year ago, Lennie and Joe were fishing on a city pier, admiring a pink and gold sunrise, when a bale of waste paper dropped from a crane during a cargo loading accident. The bale split and showered the dockside with cash that was being smuggled overseas by ship to Islamic State fighters, news reports said later. Lennie and Joe had been wearing hoodies that morning to ward off the cold, so when they stuffed the flittering banknotes inside their fish bucket and their clothes, and a plastic garbage bag, the dock's CCTV cameras couldn't identify them.

The media reported that the broken bale – one of thirty loaded, or waiting to be loaded on the *Lord of Saigon* – was linked to drug dealing by the connections of Islamic extremists and destined for shipment via South-east Asia and North Africa to Turkey and Syria. There was around $30 million in all, about $1 million in each bale. Approximately half the cash in the broken bale was recovered by the authorities on the wharf. Lennie and Joe escaped with $200,000-odd. But the investigating coppers put it out to the media that the unidentified thieves made off with $500,000. So Lennie and Joe figured the coppers took $300,000 for themselves and then tried to stiff the *mystery fishermen* with swiping all the missing cash.

The net result was that IS and its network – or the crims who had set it up and blamed IS as a cover when the shipment was exposed – were down $30 million, and as angry as a nest of bull ants who'd been pissed on. Lennie and Joe knew from the media that IS had been smashed by Western coalition armies, the Russians, the Turks, and the Kurds in Syria and Iraq and that former IS fighters were drifting home to places like Australia, some of them disguised by having a shave and buying a foreign passport with the loot they had pilfered.

Of course, these highly-skilled throat-slashers wanted to live well while they cooked up fresh ways to fuck other peoples' lives – and this required more money. Robbing banks or the like would attract tremendous attention from massively-resourced State law enforcement, so working over the so-called *criminal underworld* was smarter in the short-term, while they built towards a big-bang to celebrate their homecomings.

Lennie and Joe had discussed this *socio-political* backdrop, a term that Lennie had looked up on the internet and tried to explain to Joe, who said that he sort-of got it. In the wash-up, they had rigged some precautions in their small house, precautions which Lennie regarded as the equivalent of old-fashioned bear pits with sharpened wooden spikes pegged into their bottoms. There were just no actual pits or spikes in their inner-city Sydney address. A mixture of chemicals, hand-held combat devices, and carefully-orchestrated electrical systems was the go. Plus a bit of wit based upon experience of the unexpected.

*

Now, in the kitchen, the two friends – who had discovered an extra-sensory-perception of each other during childhood and who regarded themselves as Yin and Yang inside a single, currently thirty-three-year-old cell – felt a worm of sorts turning inside the shared psychic liver of their lives, due to the fact there

was a real-looking gun pointing at them. They knew they needed
to pluck the worm out with speed but not haste, lest they damage
themselves irreparably during the operation.

"We don't have the money," said Lennie, shaking his head,
smiling apologetically. He was telling the truth: over the past
year, they had anonymously given away or spent virtually every
dollar they had scooped from the dock, most lately on a kids'
library at Pauline's refuge.

"Where the fuck is it then?" said big hardhat.

"Word on the street says it's spread around," said Joe.

"It's what?" said hardhat, his brow furrowing. "You're talking
like it's peanut fucking butter."

"Na. Like seeds," said Joe, taking inspiration from a pink
cactus with a green knob head that was growing on the kitchen
windowsill. "You know the song...*from little things, big things
grow...*"

Hardhat groaned as if he was dealing with idiots. "What? So
you galahs invested it?"

"Look," said Joe, who picked up the teapot. "Why don't we
all have a cuppa tea and sort this out."

"I hate fucking tea," said hardhat.

"That's alright," said Joe. "I'll put some coffee on too."

Lennie motioned a welcoming hand at the oval-shaped table
that sat in the middle of the kitchen. "Please, take a seat." Lennie
took the lead and sat at one end of the table. "We might be able
to scratch each other's backs here."

Hardhat growled but sat opposite Lennie, keeping his gun
aimed at Lennie's chest.

The shoveler sat with his back to the nearest wall, a sinewy paw grasping the long handle of his tool, its glistening blade topside. He spun its head a few times and eyed Joe as if he could slice his neck in the blink of an eye. The woman sat beside the shoveler and put her tube on the table. She popped the end-cap and shook out the handle and part of the shiny steel blade of a rapier. She gripped the handle, clearly keen to show her hosts that she wasn't a simple water worker.

"Mate," Lennie said to hardhat, "It's very hard to talk sensibly to someone wearing sunnies. It's like trying to yak with a tinted window. Do you mind?"

"You two have got a right little faggot warren set up here," said hardhat, glancing at Joe's floral-patterned apron as he poured boiling water in the teapot. But the man took his sunglasses off, and his sidekicks followed suit.

Joe put three chunky white mugs in front of his guests – he wasn't trusting them with Aunty D's heirloom china – and poured them coffee from the plunger pot. He glanced at the flicking second-hand of the clock on the kitchen wall.

"Help yourselves to milk and sugar," said Joe, placing a bowl, spoons, and a jug of milk on the table.

Joe leaned against the kitchen bench and sipped tea from a delicate cup and saucer, his little finger poking up like a dog's tail. "Ah," he said as if he was doing a TV ad for a heavenly brew.

"Sounds like you've wet your pants, big feller," said hardhat, winking at his colleagues, who chuckled. Hardhat put several teaspoons of sugar in his coffee and stirred.

Joe grinned as their guests sipped. Lennie glanced at the dome-shaped fire alarm on the kitchen ceiling, specifically at the black-glass eye in its centre.

Lennie said, "You do know that the coppers lied about how much money was spilled on that wharf. They reckoned five hundred thousand went missing."

"We know that you Muppet," said hardhat, waving his gun. "We want the other two hundred thousand. Your fucking stash."

"How can you be so sure about any stash?" said Lennie. "I mean. Who *are* you people?"

"Listen, bullethead!" hardhat growled. "If we don't get the money you stole, I'll stuff that cactus over there so far up your smartarse you'll be giving birth to the pricks. That's all you need to know."

Lennie detected *mixed metaphors* balled up somewhere inside hardhat's threat about spiky plants and male and female body parts, a stuff-up with language that he'd read about in a book called *English for Dummies*. But now wasn't the time for that sort of lesson: he had another in mind, and patience was required.

Joe soft-stepped to the table and topped up his guests' coffees.

Hardhat gulped his brew and waved his gun. "There's an accountant that went missing last year too. A guy called Michael O'Hay. He stole a lot of dough off his clients. Cashed it into gold bars. There's a story going 'round that you boneheads are connected somehow. So me and my friends, we're going to have a good stickybeak through your house this morning."

"Ooh. That's embarrassing," said Joe, who was putting raspberry jam biscuits on a plate. "I haven't made the beds yet." He wondered if he was overegging his act, but every bit of gibberish he uttered served the purpose of cooking time. He patted his apron and looked at the wall clock.

Hardhat grinned. "You pillow biters are not what I expected. You remind me of a nursery rhyme."

"We're all ears," said Joe, glancing at the second hand. "Aren't we, Lennie?"

"Like elephants," Lennie replied.

Hardhat looked puzzled.

"Your nursery rhyme?" said Joe.

Hardhat's head wobbled. "Fatty and Skinny went to bed. Fatty rolled over and Skinny was dead."

"You fool!" screeched Rawcus.

Hardhat put his glassy eyes on the bird. "What did that thing say?"

Lennie raised his eyebrows apologetically. "The little feller grew up in a pub. Hears something once and you never know when he's gonna fire it back at you."

Joe put the bickie plate on the table in front of the seated woman, unable to take his gaze off her fuzzy moustache. Then it came to him. Yeah...the female Mexican artist whose paintings Lennie had taken him to see at the art gallery. Small pictures, but absolute crackers with A-grade colours. Frida someone; Joe couldn't remember her last name. He said to the woman, who apart from the mo, looked nothing like Frida's self-portraits, "Do you like to paint?"

She looked at Joe, baffled, foggy-eyed – and fell face-first onto the edge of the plate, squashing her nose and flipping her hard-hat onto the floor. Blood began seeping from the nostrils of her motionless head, pooling in the plate and staining the biscuits. Her sword in its tube fell to the floor.

"Whad the fug!" groaned big hardhat, who sounded like he'd had a dentist's needle of anesthetic plunged into his tongue. He tried to stand, wobbled, and fell back to sitting.

Joe stood behind big hardhat and head-locked him, grasping the wrist of his gun-toting hand.

Lennie pulled from its hiding place on a metal clip under the table a brass knuckleduster. He slipped it over the fingers of his left hand, intending to drive his fist into the jaw of the shovel carrier. But the man's eyes seemed to be staring at nothing, drawing sympathy from Lennie, as well as a desire to conserve energy. Lennie nudged the man's upper arm: he tumbled, his skull clunking the floor with a horrible crack.

Ka-pow!

Joe's ears were ringing from the gunshot squeezed off by big hardhat, which had missed Lennie. But he watched Rawcus fall from his swing and his body clip the edge of the kitchen work-bench before thudding to the floor, followed by a dusting of white feathers.

Rawcus lay motionless in pooling blood...

2 - LOVE

On the other side of the city...

A NAKED MAN slid low on the sofa in his beachside apartment, his legs splayed on the glass-topped coffee table in front of him, a laptop balanced on his hard belly. He Googled *LovingLife.com*, logged in, and opened a page filled with text and photos. He put spectacles on and read his profile.

My name is Will. I'm 42 years old. I'm a single dad with a daughter, Helen, aged 11.

I own my own home. I like to travel. But with a child, even though she doesn't live with me full-time, it's hard to get away as often as I'd like to our beach house. I enjoy surfing – I ride a longboard. I like dining out, going to the movies, and live music. I like pretty much any music, but not heavy metal - or opera!

I'm looking for a female companion. You don't have to have children. But other kids for Helen to play with would be great.

He nodded, pleased with the words. But he might re-edit the photo; his eyes looked a little dark around the rims, as if they were hiding something.

He stood and walked his lanky frame across a cream-carpeted sitting room onto the adjoining, cream-tiled kitchen floor, and extracted a bottle of beer from the grey fridge. A bell dinged. It reminded him of the ringer on a kid's bike. His hook on *LovingLife.com* had attracted another bite.

Returning to the sofa, he put his beer on the coffee table and propped the laptop on his thighs so he could tap the keyboard easily. On the new dating service he was testing, there was a message from a stranger named Carol.

Hi Will. I read your profile and thought we might get along. I'm divorced with a 12-year-old daughter. I love the beach. I hope you like my photo.

He studied her picture. Carol wasn't much to look at, a bit too dry-haired and thin-faced for him. But her eyes showed promise; there was a longing in them. And at least she didn't seem to be doing what others had done. The last woman he connected with had posted a picture that made her look like Angelina Jolie from *Lara Croft: Tomb Raider*. When they met for a cocktail, the woman looked more like one of his mother's prune-faced, alcoholic friends.

He typed: *Hello, Carol. Thanks for your message. Please tell me more about yourself, if you're OK with that. I'm sending you a recent photo of my daughter and me. All the best, Will.* He uploaded a newly made family snap.

She replied: *It's a lovely photo. Here's one of Donna and me.*

Yes, he said to himself as he looked at Carol's and Donna's images. They would do nicely.

Will: *Where do you live, Carol? I'm in Bondi.*

Carol: *I'm not that lucky. I'm in Summer Hill.*

Will: *Would you like to meet for coffee?*

Carol: *Sounds terrific.*

They set a date and place. He stepped across the room and looked through glass, floor-to-ceiling balcony doors over the road to the ocean. He slid a door open and savoured the salty air. The breeze was blowing offshore, the morning sun was shining, and head-high waves were peeling right off the reef beside the rocky headland of the bay.

Dr Ross Fellows, PhD, thought that he might actually buy a surfboard one day.

3 - DEAD OR ALIVE

JOE DIALLED UP his armlock on big hardhat's neck, the restriction of blood and oxygen causing the man's body to go rubbery. Joe pulled the gun from his gurgling captive's fingers and said, "Shush!"

The phone on the kitchen wall was ringing.

It went to voice mail. Pauline Gerrity said: *Carol has made first contact. Please call me A-S-A-P.*

"Rawcus!" Joe yelled to Lennie, who was trying to drag a plastic bin bag over the head of the shovel carrier, who was writhing on the floor like a cut snake.

"We'll get to him in a sec," said Lennie, who had a decent wrestle on his hands. After nudging the man off the chair and stunning him with the head clunk on the slate-tiled floor, Lennie had grabbed the wire that connected his laptop to his mouse and attempted to tie the man's hands behind his back. But for a person who had a shitload of horse tranquiliser in his bloodstream from drinking Joe's Ketamine-laced coffee and sugar, the shovel carrier was pretty good at shaking his head and keeping it out of the plastic bag. Survival instinct never ceased to amaze Lennie.

Joe flipped off hardhat's helmet using the muzzle of the gun – and hammered the base of the pistol grip on the man's crown. Hardhat squealed. Joe knew that spot hurt like hell. It's where his old headmaster, Mr Darian, used to rap his knuckles on Joe's skull before he ordered Joe into his office and taught him what an anatomically inquisitive eel from the Grade 5 aquarium could do to a boy.

Joe released hardhat's neck; the man swayed in his seat like he'd downed a bottle of whisky in thirty seconds flat.

Lennie was sick of wrestling. He grabbed the shoveler by the hair, lifted his head, and slammed a temple into the floor, followed by an encore which subdued the shoveler quite a lot, enabling Lennie to slip the bag over the man's head and knot the handles under his chin. Applying the knot reminded Lennie of securing a scarf to his demented gran's head to take her for night walks, sky-gazing, while she told him tales about flying inside the Milky Way and the friends she met there, including a bus-sized, white wombat named Max.

The recall of Max prompted Lennie to regret smoking the joint earlier, although it was proving to be a bloody good batch; the only problem being the timing of its ingestion and the duration of its effect on his synapses. The plastic bag on the shoveler's head inflated and deflated, making a crackling noise.

"You'll suv-ogate 'im," moaned big hardhat, fighting not to fall from the chair.

"He'll last a minute or two," said Lennie. "About as long as you."

At the threat of a shortened lifespan, hardhat rallied and began rising, so Joe thumped the pistol grip on the man's crown again, applying extra ferocity at the sight of dead Rawcus. The man's eyeballs orbited in their sockets like those of the dolls that Joe had just purchased to give to kids at Pauline's refuge.

"I'm nod veeling doo vell," the man groaned, blood trickling from splits in two purple eggs that were growing on top of his skull through combed-over, black-dyed hair.

Lennie put his face so close to the eyes of the home invader that he could smell the man's garbage truck breath and said, "That's how you're meant to feel."

"You've killed Rawcus," growled Joe, tucking the pistol into the front waist of his jeans before lifting their motionless cockatoo from the floor, cradling the bird in his hands like a sleeping baby. Rawcus's head flopped and Joe gently arranged his feathered neck into the curve of an arm.

Lennie pulled the leather belt from his jeans and kneed hardhat in the ribs, knocking him from the chair to the floor where he landed in a foetal position that annoyed Lennie, not because of the fundamental shape but because the shaper seemed to be playing with Lennie's heartstrings by posing as an innocent.

Lennie rolled the fat man onto his back, then kneeled beside him. He dragged hardhat by his collars and propped his head and neck against a thick leg of the kitchen table. Lennie's belt had buckle holes punched intermittently along its entire length, not because Lennie thought he might become incredibly skinny one day, but because it made the belt incredibly versatile. He wrapped the leather strap around the man's throat and the table leg, lacing the tongue through the buckle and pulling it so tight that hardhat could only gurgle and claw at the belt.

"No wanking," Lennie said.

"What about her?" said Joe, running his fingers gently over a white wing that was stained with a growing scarlet patch.

Fuzzy-mo was still seated at the table, motionless, her face planted nose-down on the plate of biscuits.

Lennie put a couple of his fingers to the jugular vein in her neck. "She's alive."

Joe's eyes were watery. He held Rawcus to his cheek, feeling for body heat. Then he listened to the feathered torso like it was a telephone handset. "There's a heartbeat! We need to get him to a vet."

"Hang on," said Lennie. "Let's think."

"What's to think, mate? He's taken a bullet. We might save him."

Lennie scanned the kitchen: blood was dripping from Rawcus down Joe's sky blue T-shirt; the man with the plastic bag on his head had stopped writhing and the bag was barely moving; hardhat was fighting against his sedation, trying half-heartedly to stick his fingers between the belt and his throat; fuzzy-mo was snoring at the table, sniffling now and then; Bruce was chewing his rat on the step, his deafness and partial blindness sheltering him from the storm that had raged in the kitchen, though Lennie often wondered if Bruce's senses were selective.

Lennie wished he could be selective with his own perceptions right now, but taking some tasty drugs wasn't going to clean this mess up.

He looked at Joe. "How are we going to explain to the vet how Rawcus got shot?"

Joe looked inside his brain for the thing called *logic* that he'd learned about in his last adult literacy class.

Lennie's phone trilled inside his jeans pocket, and he dug it out. The name *Pauls* lit the screen. It might be an emergency.

"Lennie," said Pauline Gerrity. "Did you get my voice message about Carol on your house phone? I thought you must be out."

"Got it," he replied. "But Joe and I are a bit tied up at the mo'. So you keep that show on the road, and we'll come back to you A-sap. It might be twenty-four hours or so."

"Anything I can help with?"

Lennie looked at Joe, who had Rawcus on the bench and was gently wrapping his torso with a bandage. Pauline was an A-grade helper and the smartest person he'd ever met, but her being confined to a wheelchair affected her speed to a scene. Most of all, this was their mess, not hers. "Na, Pauls, thanks. We're good. Gotta go."

"Mrs Giannopoulos," Lennie called to Joe, who flashed a thumbs up.

4 - THE RAT AND THE CHEESE

CHILD PSYCHOLOGIST, Dr Ross Fellows, PhD, phoned his workplace and asked the office co-ordinator to cancel his afternoon appointments, explaining that he'd been struck down by a sudden-onset gastric bug that he did not want to risk passing on to his colleagues. He showered, shaved, and dressed in a light blue suit with an open-necked white shirt.

Standing in front of a full-length bedroom mirror, the doctor admired the image he had created of love-seeking single father, *Will Carter,* on *Lovinglife.com.* He presented as fit but not slick, a man in his early forties who was health-conscious and well-groomed. Fellows looked for it but he could see no narcissism in his reflection and was pleased. His phone beeped: an Uber driver was on approach to his Bondi flat for the ride to The Horizon café in the inner Sydney suburb of Surry Hills where he would meet Carol. He had been more than happy with her suggested venue, which was easy walking distance from the city's central railway station to which she could easily catch a train from her home.

Carol had not been too proud to admit that on her single mother's budget, she had no car and relied on public transport. Financial vulnerability, while not a central component of his planned experiment with Carol, was helpful, and it reinforced his view that he was on the right track with her as subject matter.

In the Uber, the driver asked Fellows if he would like to read *The Guardian* newspaper from London. The driver's previous pick-up from the international airport had left it in his car. Fellows, being a cosmopolitan man, accepted the offer, but on glancing at the front-page story he cast the paper aside as if it might be harbouring a contagious disease.

The main item was about an American billionaire named Jeffrey Epstein, who had committed suicide in prison while facing charges of grooming and sexually abusing underage girls. The article threw new light on Epstein's relationships with Britain's Prince Andrew, and former US Presidents, Donald Trump and Bill Clinton, as well as other well-heeled guests at Epstein's mansions. But the thing that made Fellows' eyes pop was a sidebar story that suggested Epstein had a stake in a Chinese factory that produced inflatable dolls of children.

"Are you alright, sir?" asked the driver, glancing into the rear-view mirror. "Looks like you've seen a ghost."

"I don't believe in ghosts," Fellows insisted, patting his cheeks to encourage the return of blood. "I'm a rationalist." He took a mini-bottle of sanitiser from his trouser pocket and washed his hands.

The grinning driver glanced again at Fellows. "You're not a TV journalist, are you sir?"

"Afraid not."

"Oh? I could swear I've seen you on the news."

Fellows ignored him.

The driver said, "I've got a feeling you're going to be famous one day, sir."

"Psychic are you?"

"My mum reckons I am. Though she's been dead for years." The driver smiled.

Fellows made a mental note to give the driver a zero-star rating.

On arrival at the café, Fellows chose a table on the footpath. He smiled at the arriving waitperson with lips so peeled back, with gums so exposed, and with teeth so white that the combined effect appeared to shock the menu-bearing girl, who pulled back sharply.

"I'm waiting for a friend," he said, adjusting his lips over his teeth, unsure where to stop them, telling himself he needed to get back in front of the mirror and work on his sincerity.

*

Across the street from The Horizon, behind a tinted-glass door on a balcony above a convenience store, Carol surveyed her man with binoculars.

"So," said a fair-haired, young woman sitting in a wheelchair beside Carol. "Tell me your legend again."

"Surname, Simpson. I'm a registered nurse," said Carol, handing the binoculars to her companion. "I'm employed by an agency that places staff in temporary vacancies in hospitals across Sydney. But I mainly work in the inner west because I live in rented rooms in Summer Hill, and it's easier for me to get to work locally. I'm currently employed at the Strathfield Private Hospital, caring for people in surgical recovery."

"Kids?" said Pauline Gerrity.

"My daughter Donna is twelve-years-old. She is in year six at Summer Hill Primary School. She plays soccer and netball."

"Her father?"

"Working in the mines in Western Australia somewhere, I believe. He dumped Donna and me five years ago, and I haven't heard from him since. He has skipped his child maintenance payments. But I'm glad *not* to have contact with him because of his use of drugs and violence, to both my daughter and me."

"Your parents?"

"They live in Brisbane. My dad's a plumber. Mum is a dress-maker."

They practised other details about her siblings, family history and friends, old schools, old jobs, her simple ambitions for a stable home, and a sober, gentle father-figure for Donna.

Pauline said, "Well done, darling."

"My nerves aren't helping," said Carol, who held up a shaking hand.

"Par for the course on a first date," said Pauline, waving the binoculars. "Just remember. I'll be watching you with these. And my friends are a phone call away." She hoped this was true, and that whatever emergency Lennie and Joe were dealing with would be resolved speedily in their favour.

"What if he invites me on to somewhere else?"

"Can't make it. You're doing an evening shift tonight."

Carol finger-combed her shoulder-length, chestnut-coloured hair and refreshed her lipstick in front of a wall mirror before she opened the front door and stepped into the hallway. She travelled by lift to an underground car park and used a fire exit to enter the laneway behind Pauline's flat.

At the lane's intersection with a side-street, she walked uphill to the main thoroughfare of Crown Street, where there was a set of traffic lights. The Horizon café was straight across the street on the corner. As she waited for the lights to turn green, she saw him at the table. He smiled and waved, and she waved back. Her legs went rubbery at thoughts of what she knew about him, but she was able to get them to carry her body in its navy-blue and white-polka-dot dress across the street.

5 - THE DREAMING CHAIR

"IT'S LENNIE here, Mrs G...No, it wasn't a party popper...we have an emergency...No, no. It's Rawcus. A gunshot wound...yeah, best you do the three monkeys on this one...OK, good idea. We'll use the bedroom door."

Joe shuffled beside him, cradling Rawcus whom he'd wrapped lightly in a bath towel with just his sulphur-crested head protruding. His eyes and beak remained closed.

Lennie said to Joe, "Mrs G has relatives over. Old ones, thankfully, who can't use stairs."

"I'm on it," said Joe, who stepped across the kitchen towards the staircase in the sitting room.

Lennie followed, glancing at the shovel-man on the floor. The bag over his head had stopped inflating and deflating. "Hang on," he grizzled to Joe.

Lennie grabbed a sharp pencil from a glass jar stuffed with similar tools that sat upon a kitchen dresser. He bent over the man and poked holes through the plastic around where he guessed his mouth and nose would be. "Whoops," he said, pulling out the bloodied nib.

Joe, observing that the plastic bag remained as lively as a popped balloon, said, "He needs a kick start."

"Gotcha. Cardiopulmonary," said Lennie. "You go. I'll deal with this."

Joe stepped into the sitting room and called back, "Let's use the electric chair on this lot!"

"Top idea!"

Lennie pressed his boot upon the shoveler's chest as if he was working the foot pump on a blow-up mattress. The plastic bag started puffing and de-puffing. He heard Joe's big feet clumping up the creaking staircase.

*

On the first-floor landing, Joe turned right. At the second door along the corridor, he punched the numbers *7-9-5* into a key-pad on a wall by the frame. *Click. Hiss.* He stepped through the vacuum-sealed entrance into blazing white light and thick, humid air. He inhaled the sweet aroma of ceiling-high Mars Grass plants that were growing in troughs of liquid nutrients.

Joe brushed past the sticky leaves to a tall mirror on the wall that they shared with Mrs G's place. There was a light switch beside the mirror. He flicked it on and off, three times. *Click. Hiss* A lock released and he slid the mirror sideways along the wall. Little Mrs G was waiting on the other side in a matching room full of plants.

"Quickly, Joe," said Mrs G, who always reminded Joe of a willy-wagtail, the way she flitted about. "Bring him through to my bathroom."

Joe placed Rawcus on the surface of a vanity beside the sink, unfurled the towel and bandage, and showed Mrs G where the bullet had sliced between wing and ribcage.

She lifted the spectacles on a chain around her neck and eyed the wound. "Sometimes there's just a millimetre between life and death, Joe."

"Which side is Rawcus on?"

"Ours." She took a pair of surgical gloves from a dispenser on the vanity and put them on.

"Why'd you give up nursing, Mrs G?"

"Too old." She lifted the wing gently away from Rawcus's torso.

"How come you're still working then?"

"In the hospital, it all turned to computers, love. Too much box-checking and not enough hands-on caring."

She lifted a stethoscope from a wall hook. She put the buds into her ears and placed the listening button on Rawcus's chest...

*

Lennie unbuckled the belt that had locked big hardhat's throat against the kitchen table leg – then wrestled with a mental challenge.

This guy was the size of a horse and as good as lame from the pistol-butt clunks on his head and restricted access to air for the last five minutes. So how was Lennie going to get hard-hat into the garden shed, where the electric chair awaited? Drag him by the ankles? Mm. Slow and messy. A thought sparked: his homemade, lithium-battery cattle prod might get the big guy moving. Mm. It could deliver erratic results: a fired-up boofhead of this size might smash the furniture and arouse the attention of less friendly neighbours than Mrs G. Mm. He settled on a third option.

"I've called an ambulance, mate," Lennie said to hardhat, dialling up the volume in his voice, figuring from the man's foggy eyes that his brain was more unconscious than conscious and that he might need amplification to get electrical impulses to jump from synapse to synapse for processing.

"Come on, let's get you on your feet. The ambo's have a chair waiting for you in the garden. It's too tricky to get it up the back step here."

"O-gay," grumbled hardhat as Lennie grabbed him by a hand, braced and pulled him to his feet, slipping his shoulder under hardhat's armpit.

"Excuse me, Bruce," said Lennie, kicking the leftovers of the cat's rat off the doorstep. Bruce followed his carcass down the footpath.

Lennie and hardhat stumbled along the narrow concrete path beside the kitchen wall and fence, Lennie using the wall as a buttress now and then to stop his man from falling. They spilled into the courtyard garden which was lined by raised beds bursting with flowers of every colour of the rainbow.

Hardhat seemed to be a flower lover. "Priddy," he mumbled.

"Yeah, pretty," said Lennie, kicking open the door of the garden shed. "In you go, mate."

"Ambo?" mumbled hardhat.

"Yep," said Lennie. "We'll just sit you down in this comfy seat here."

Hardhat fell into a paint-scratched dentist's chair. His eyes flickered; his jaw drooped.

Lennie plugged an electrical cord from the chair into a socket in the wall and flicked the switch on. He worked a foot pedal. The chair lurched from the sitting position to prone, taking hardhat's compliant body with it.

"Not ambo," gurgled hardhat.

"This is better," said Lennie, who took a pair of latex gloves from a box on a workbench and slipped his hands in. He pushed the man's buttock to one side, just enough to extract his wallet from the back pocket of his trousers. "Now, let's see who you are."

Lennie flipped the wallet open. "Oh, for fuck's sake...Ronald Arthur Tremlett. Detective Sergeant, Ronald Arthur Tremlett."

*

In Mrs G's bathroom, she lifted the stethoscope button from Rawcus's torso.

"It's nice and steady, Joe," she said. "We better get to the bleeding."

Joe helped her to spread and hold unconscious Rawcus's wing on the make-shift operating slab of paper towels on top of the vanity.

"It's not a deep wound," said Mrs G, bathing the area with a cotton swab dipped in saline solution. "It looks like the bullet grazed his breast under the wing. It's torn some tissue."

"So why is he out like a light?"

"Did he hit his head when he fell? It may be a concussion."

Joe recalled the scene in the kitchen. Rawcus did clunk his skull against the bench when he fell from his broomstick. And he had hit the floor hard.

"This is what happened to our friend Pauline Gerrity, you know," said Joe, his voice shaky. "She got knocked off a scooter, hit her head on the road, and got paralysed. Permanently."

"Let's not get ahead of ourselves, Joe."

"Can you bring him back?"

"We'll do our best, love. The first step is to clean his wound properly and stop the bleeding. We don't want him getting an infection."

Mrs G opened the double doors of a large wall cabinet.

"Hooley Dooley," said Joe, his eyes popping at the sight of dozens of bottles. "Enough colours here to make a paint chart jealous. They magic potions?"

"You could say that."

"So what do you call your job these days?"

"Herbalism and naturopathy. I use plants for healing." She lifted two small bottles and a jar from the cabinet and placed them beside Rawcus.

Joe said, "Sounds like witchcraft...*double, double toil and trouble. Fire burn and cauldron bubble.*"

"So you know Shakespeare?" said Mrs G, who opened a bottle of violet fluid. "The three witches from *Macbeth?*"

Joe winked. "Na, I'm into the classics. *Snow White.* Seen it?"

Mrs G smiled and set to work using cotton balls to dab violet on the wound under Rawcus's wing. She plugged the wound with gauze that she daubed in an amber-coloured ointment from the jar before wrapping his torso in a white bandage, and re-wrapping his whole body in a fresh cotton towel like a mother might wrap her newborn to sleep.

With Rawcus immobilised, she unscrewed a bottle cap that was attached to a glass stick upon which clear liquid glistened.

"What's that one?" said Joe.

"Smelling salts," Mrs G explained. "A mixture of ammonia, alcohol, and eucalyptus oil. A sniff might stimulate his lungs and bring him around."

Mrs G waved the stick backward and forward past the air holes in Rawcus's beak.

Rawcus's eyes flickered. One opened.

"You're a miracle worker," said Joe, stroking Rawcus's sulphur crest. "Hello, little man," he whispered.

Rawcus's other eye opened.

"Can you talk, mate?" said Joe.

Rawcus stared blankly.

"He's disoriented," said Mrs G. "He needs rest now."

"So he's out of the woods?"

"I hope so."

Joe nodded at the bottle of smelling salts. "Do you have a spare, Mrs G? Lennie and I have a situation next door, and we could use a bit of your wake-em juice."

Mrs G reached into her cupboard, but as she handed the vial to Joe, Rawcus's head began to shudder and his eyes flickered. Foam bubbled from his beak.

Joe's hands began shaking. "What's happening?"

"Convulsions, Joe. It's a symptom of medical shock."

"What does that mean?"

Mrs G put her stethoscope back on Rawcus's chest. "Oh, my," she said. "His little heart is going so fast I can't measure it."

*

Lennie paced inside his garden shed with a furrowed brow.

"Listen, Ronnie," said Lennie. "I'm just going to put these straps on you, so you don't fall out of the chair while I check on your pals."

"Fug ov," said DS Tremlett.

Lennie velcro-strapped Tremlett's wrists and forearms to the armrests of the electric chair, tightened a lap-belt on the detective that he'd recycled from an old car seat, and velcro-strapped Tremlett's shins and ankles to the leg and footrests.

When Lennie entered the kitchen, fuzzy-mo was stirring at the table, grumbling. The shoveler dozed on the floor, his headbag inflating and deflating with a steady rhythm. Lennie checked their pockets for ID but found nothing. He took a roll of gaffer tape from a cupboard and spent a few minutes wrapping the home invaders like a spider might spin thread around prey to preserve them.

He took his laptop off a kitchen bench, collected a fresh roll of tape, and returned to the shed where he put the items on a workbench. Tremlett was dozing, drool clinging to his chin. A denture had come loose in his open mouth.

Lennie figured that a man talks more clearly with secure teeth, so he used a pair of narrow-headed pliers to push the strays back into place, wanting to avoid having the yellow chompers crunch his fingers. Lennie smiled; he might soon need to go in the opposite direction and threaten to pull teeth, or drill fresh cavities, to extract reference points from Tremlett that would enable him to join the dots of the bigger picture that they were all now part of.

Alternatively, Lennie thought, he might requisition Bruce's rat, or what was left of it, and ask Tremlett if he'd prefer that down his throat, or to fess up his plot. Lennie's buzzing thoughts were interrupted by a cough behind him. He grabbed a screwdriver and spun to confront the source.

"Sheess! Never sneak up on a highly-strung man," he said.

Joe was standing in the doorway.

"Rawcus?" said Lennie.

"Touch and go, mate. He's in shock. Just had a fit."

"We better get him to the vet then, and take our chances with this lot and the coppers turning up."

"I think we can hold fire there," said Joe, wiping his red eyes with a couple of fingertips. "Mrs G is a national treasure, and she's got a team on board."

"What do you mean?"

"Can you believe this?" said Joe. "She's got a laptop in her bathroom, and she's on a live Zoom chat with an animal doctor and a helper in the United States who're mates of hers."

"So they're fixing him?"

"She's got more medicines in her cupboards than that Chemist Warehouse up the street. If there's an emergency, she'll call us. She said not to worry."

"Are you worried?" said Lennie, who reached into his jeans pocket and touched a little-finger-shaped carving of Bloodwood tree that he called a Lucky Jack.

Joe nodded at the man in the chair. "So who's fatso?"

"Ah, tricky. He's a copper. A detective sergeant, no less."

"Shit. Division?"

"Armed Robbery. I'm guessing he's connected to those thieving plods who nicked that three hundred grand off the wharf and tried to pin it on the *mystery fishermen*."

"Whatta we do?"

Lennie massaged his jaw. "We need to wake this prick up and extract some intelligence, if it exists. There's no ID on those sleepers in the kitchen."

"This might help," said Joe, pulling the bottle of Mrs G's smelling salts from his jeans pocket. "It snapped Rawcus out of a coma. Briefly anyway."

"I was going to use this," Lennie said, plucking a small bottle off a shed shelf.

"Mm. Amyl nitrate," said Joe. " I reckon it's cocktail hour."

"I reckon you're right," said Lennie, who took a rag from a wall hook, screwed the top off the amyl bottle, and shook the fluid onto the rag. "I better do a tester, to make sure it's not past its use-by date." Lennie sniffed the rag; his eyes went as wide as poached eggs. "Gad-zooga!"

Joe took the rag from Lennie and shook his liquid smelling salts onto it. Lennie hit the rag again with splashes of amyl – and Joe thrust the fuming cloth over Tremlett's nose and mouth. Moments passed.

Tremlett's body shuddered as if there was an earthquake building inside him; his eyes flashed open, their glassy pink balls trying to leap out of his skull.

"Fucking monsters!" cried Tremlett.

"Na. It's just us," replied Lennie, who took the roll of tape off the bench, realising he needed to gaffer Tremlett's skull into the chair's head braces to stop him flicking about. He screwed the earmuff-style braces tight against Tremlett's temples and applied the tape across his forehead with several turns.

"Right," said Lennie, pressing his boot on the foot pedal to bend the chair up to the sitting position. "Do you like home entertainment, Ronnie?"

"What?" said an exceedingly bright-eyed Tremlett.

Lennie opened his laptop on the bench in front of Tremlett and clicked a few buttons. "Joe, give Ronnie another blast of your potion, will you? We don't want him missing any of the action."

Joe ragged Tremlett. When the detective's breathing had slowed a little, Lennie hit *play* on a video. It relayed sight and sound of the gathering earlier in the kitchen, in which Tremlett, disguised as a *Sydney Water* worker, was waving a gun and making death threats about stolen money.

Tremlett looked bewildered.

Lennie said, "Camera in the kitchen ceiling."

"Sneaky fuckers," growled Tremlett.

"You know what I reckon, Ronnie?" said Lennie. "*You* are doing a bit of freelancing today. You've jumped the leash. You are not here on official business, or you'd have shown us your badge. So this video would prove very interesting to your bosses, and the media. We'd edit ourselves out, of course."

"You're a dead man, Larsen," Tremlett spat, scowling at Joe. "And your pet gorilla."

"Who are those friends of yours sleeping in our kitchen?" said Lennie.

"Fuck yourself. I'm the law."

"Not here, Ronnie. Not here."

Lennie looked at Joe. "Mate, can you get the party kit from the house?"

Joe left the shed.

"You know, Ronnie," said Lennie, flicking for the sound effect the wrists of the latex gloves he was wearing before picking up an electric drill from the workbench. "There were a couple of other big men who threatened us recently. They said if we didn't give them what they wanted, they'd turn our testicles into Swiss cheese with one of these."

Lennie inserted a drill bit as long as a pencil. "Am I getting your attention, egghead?"

Tremlett appeared to absorb the subliminal implant. He moaned, "My head hurts."

Lennie triggered the drill and waved its mechanical whine. "I can help you there, mate. Heard of trepanning?"

"Huh?"

"Goes way back. The ancient Greeks were into. See, someone drills a hole in your skull, right through the bone. Meant to cure seizures, madness, and headaches. Want to try?"

"Fuck you, weasel."

Lennie put the whirling bit close to Tremlett's ear. "Who sent you lot?"

Tremlett spluttered, "You'll get twenty years for this, you dumb prick. You're in deep shit."

"Good point," said Lennie, pulling back to avoid the spittle. "Going down this path could get very fucking messy. And I'm not much into cleaning."

Joe stepped into the shed hugging under an arm a wine-bottle-sized gas canister connected to a clear plastic tube and a face mask. His other hand clutched a sunglasses case. He put the items on the bench in front of Tremlett.

"Now, we have a few muck-less options here to bring about the free-flow of information," said Lennie. "Think of them like mental enemas."

"What are you talking about, you five-star idiot?"

Lennie smiled. "Joe, will you do the honours?"

Joe opened the hinged sunglasses case and extracted a plastic syringe to which he attached a steel tip. He took out a small bottle of clear fluid, inserted the tip through the rubber seal, and drew the syringe about half full. Tremlett wriggled hard, "No! Pleease."

"Let me see," said Lennie, browsing the internet on his laptop screen. "Ah, yes. Here we are. *Ketamine...is a medication mainly used for starting and maintaining anaesthesia. It induces a trance-like state...common side effects may include agitation, confusion, or hallucinations.*"

Joe placed the syringe on the bench, stepped to Tremlett's side, and pushed up his shirtsleeve.

Tremlett said, "OK, OK! For fuck's sake. They are my fellow officers. We are working undercover to retrieve the money from the dock and track the connected terrorist network. The best thing you guys can do now is let me free. If we get the money back, we are all sweet and square. I mean, you have that video from your kitchen, right? So if you don't stuff us up, we won't stuff you up. All good. Yeah?"

"Jesus, Ronnie. You lie your way into our home, shoot our bird, and now you spout this bullshit."

"It's not bullshit."

"Joe," said Lennie. "I reckon we go the barbecue gas."

"You'll rot for life in prison if you kill me," cried Tremlett. "Help!"

Joe kicked the shed door shut. He grasped the gas canister in one hand and used his other to turn the outlet valve on. Gas hissed into the facemask.

"You murdering fu...," groaned Tremlett as Joe pressed the mask over his mouth and nose.

Joe grinned as the look on Tremlett's face went from horror, like he was about to have his bowels sliced open and intestines ripped out, to a sort-of drooling teenage pleasure as if he was on the verge of orgasm.

"Do you like that, Mr Tremlett?" said Joe.

"Are you with us, Ronnie?" said Lennie, who nodded at Joe to remove the mask for a bit.

Joe was careful to hide from Tremlett's gaze the sticker on the gas bottle that said N2O. The laughing gas was one of half a dozen bottles that were an off-the-books, side-deal with the dentist who sold them his old chair.

Taking in the dopy look on Tremlett's face, Joe recalled that after his own few lungs full of nitrous oxide, shit movies on the TV had looked way better.

Joe smiled, recalling that Lennie, after he'd had a decent sniff, had a brainwave for a new business that involved gassing entire cinemas. The stuff was odourless and Lennie figured they could patent and sell the rights to a theatre chain or two, which would have audiences flocking back into their venues, even to Aussie movies, which hardly anyone wanted to see these days. The technology could flow on to pubs and music places, cafés even, so Lennie reckoned. Any space where you could shut a door and trap a crowd. The potential was infinite. It just needed some creative entrepreneurship and an appetite for risk. Though when the first bottle of gas ran out, Lennie's enthusiasm drifted away too.

"How does your head feel?" said Lennie, tapping the electric chair's foot pedal to make Tremlett prone. "Pain gone on holiday, amigo?"

Tremlett smiled. "Are we in Barcelona?"

Lennie sat on a crate with his mouth close to Tremlett's ear. He felt like a psychiatrist talking to a patient, like one of those old-fashioned shrinks he'd seen on black and white films who had proper couches and mysterious lighting. Those were the days, he thought. These days, when Lennie went to see his court-ordered psych, he got to sit in a boring chair in a boring room, so it was no wonder those sessions were useless. Create a moody set, then you'll get a meaningful result, he reminded himself.

"Let's start again, old chum," he said to Tremlett. "Who are the people in my kitchen?"

"Ah, Lennie boy. That's for me to know and you to find out."

"Do you want more gas, Ronnie?"

Tremlett nodded.

"Well," said Lennie. "Sharing is a two-way street."

"She," said Tremlett, "is the step-sister of the Enoka brothers. Nancy."

"Well, I'll be," said Lennie, rolling his eyes at Joe. "Give Ronnie a treat."

The fucking Enokas, thought Joe, as he positioned the mask on Tremlett's face. There were once five of the big Pacific

Islanders cruising around Sydney. Three of them were dead; he and Lennie knew that for sure. But the other two, the twins Chris and John? A while ago, he and Lennie had left the non-swimmers clinging to a lifebuoy in Sydney Harbour, after which they had sicked the Australian Federal Police onto the brothers with pretty good evidence that they were fund-raising for Islamic State terrorists, and doing freelance jobs for neo-Nazi white supremacists as if to prove they were men of even morals. But their current location was a mystery. And a worry.

"So, Ronnie," said Lennie. "The shoveler. Who's he?"

Tremlett laughed as Joe pulled the mask away. "Too funny, mate. It's too funny."

"Try us," said Lennie.

"He's my brother-in-law."

"How funny is that?" Lennie said in monotone to Joe, who eyed the Ketamine kit thinking he'd like to give Tremlett the same treatment that vets gave horses with broken legs.

"No, no," said Tremlett. "There's a punchline." Tremlett sniffed loudly at Joe and nodded at the mask. "Do you mind?"

Joe re-gassed him. "Ta, bro," said Tremlett. "Now, the bro-in-law. He's deaf, mate. Like your fucking cat."

"Wow," said Lennie.

"It gets better," said Tremlett, chuckling. "He's mute too. Can't speak. Lost his tongue to cancer."

Tremlett made a ga-ga sound that seemed to mock the tongueless man. "And the poor cunt is illiterate. Can barely write his own name." Tremlett cackled.

"Oh," said Joe. "That's hilarious, Mr Tremlett. Do you know, I couldn't read or write until about a year ago? Now I'm in adult learning."

"Come to think of it," said Tremlett, "you do look like a dumb cunt. Down Syndrome, is it?"

"Are you married, Mr Tremlett?" Joe replied.

"Are you kidding, Downy? I'm in my prime. You know...why buy a book when you can fuck the whole library for free?"

"Just wondering if there's a wife and kids who might benefit."

"From what?"

Joe put the gas bottle on the floor by his feet. "Your life insurance."

"Oh, come on, Downy boy!" said Tremlett, dribbling. "You're far too serious. I love you, mate. Just a dash more, hey?"

Lennie turned to Joe and said, "I've got an idea. Can you re-Ket him? While you're doing that, I'll ring TC. We could use an extra hand for a few hours. Someone with his tech skills."

6 - BOOBY TRAPS

JOE PEERED through a fish-eye security lens at a pretty face.

The Chemist could pass for a young teenager, boy or girl. But he identified as male and claimed to be twenty-seven years of age. Joe opened the front door.

"Thanks for coming, TC," said Joe, glancing into the street for signs of the surviving Enokas brothers, or a rescue party from big hardhat's possibly extended gang. All he saw was Mrs G who was waving away a grey-haired couple who were driving along the footpath in matching electric buggies with green reflector flags atop whip poles. The couple played dodgem cars, bumping wheels, leading Joe to wonder if they'd been doing more than drinking tea with Mrs G. He shut the door behind TC.

TC's ski-slope nose could have slotted into Joe's belly button if either man was in the mood for a hug. They weren't.

The scientist was wearing his trademark navy-blue, leather-tasselled boat shoes; cream-coloured chinos with a centre crease; and a tucked-in, short-sleeved white polo shirt over biceps that always reminded Joe of peeled, soft-boiled eggs. As always, he combed his short, fair hair with a side-part. Yeah, thought Joe, TC was the spitting image of a boy-girl he'd seen on the cover of a magazine called *Frankie* in the surgery of the dentist who had provided their electric chair.

Joe squinted at TC. "Mate, did you buy that outfit as a job lot?"

"What do you mean?"

"You always wear the same stuff, but it never gets old, or dirty."

"Economies of scale, Joe. Buy in bulk and you get a discount. And when you're on a good thing, what do you do?"

"Come meet our guests," said Joe, who led TC into the kitchen and pointed at the bloody-nosed woman who was now dozing laying on the floor, her wrists and ankles trussed with tape. "Say hello to Nancy. She's a step-sister of the Enoka brothers, apparently."

"Shit," said TC taking a couple of steps back, his eyes popping as if he'd stumbled upon a poisonous snake.

Joe felt for TC. It wasn't so long ago that he and Lennie had peeled open a tarp covering the back tray of a small truck owned by Chris Enoka. Under the tarp, they discovered TC – stripped to his singlet and underpants, with his spine bent backward like a boomerang because his wrists and ankles were hog-tied behind him. He'd been rendered mute by a stylish gag: a blue rubber ball was locked in his mouth by a contraption made of white leather straps with silver buckles.

Lennie at the unveiling had declared that TC looked like "a designer handbag for psychos". And after being untied, TC confirmed that Chris Enoka had, in fact, carried him around by one hand using the hog-tie-ropes as a handle.

"Where's Rawcus?" said TC, looking up at the empty broomstick.

"Long story I'll cut short," said Joe, who beat the urge for a cold beer and drank a glass of water while he briefed TC on the day's events.

"So he's in intensive care?" said TC.

"He's in good hands," said Joe, who sketched Lennie's vision for this afternoon and the early evening.

*

Lennie stepped up off the garden path and through the kitchen doorway. "Ah," he said on seeing TC, "Donna Simpson has arrived."

"I'm not sure I can pull it off, Lennie," said TC. "Dressing up as a schoolgirl. It's too weird."

"OK. That's for later. We have to tidy up this clusterfuck first. Has Joe given you the plan?"

"Yes."

"You better put these on," said Lennie, handing TC a pair of flesh-coloured surgical gloves. "You need to find our visitors' car."

"How?"

"Take this," said Lennie, throwing TC an electronic key he'd found in Tremlett's satchel. "Just walk up and down the street and punch the button until lights flash on something sitting on four wheels."

"I have a first-class, post-doctoral degree in biochemistry, Lennie. I think I can work that out."

"I'd forgotten you were a genius."

TC blushed.

Lennie said, "When you find their chariot, see if there's anything dangerous in there. Because we are going to take it for a drive."

TC's eyebrows shot up. "Do you mean booby traps? Like spring-loaded seat spikes? Or a poison-gas burglar device?"

Lennie could relate to TC's paranoid streak, it was partly why he liked him, but now wasn't the time to play with it.

"I'm thinking more like cameras, or GPS trackers. And Joe? Can you drive Firefly into the lane? We need to load these carcasses before their friends send a posse."

Joe and TC stepped out the front door into the street.

Lennie dragged by the ankles along the kitchen floor the taped-up and freshly-Ketamined Nancy, who Joe had dosed orally through an eyedropper, given she didn't seem to have much tolerance for the stuff.

Lennie left her snoring in the courtyard and went back for the shoveler. He felt a tad sorry for the man as he dragged him. The poor tongueless bastard couldn't speak, couldn't hear, couldn't read, couldn't write. Even if he could do sign language, he was a slave to Tremlett, and God knows what his relationship was with Nancy Enoka. Still, the bloke had entered their home uninvited and armed with a sharp blade and bad intent – and Lennie intended to make sure that neither this trio nor its mates ever returned. But this objective raised a new problem: the negative aspect of having a permanent home made of bricks and mortar.

The positive aspect, Lennie reminded himself, was that a fixed address gave you stability, like the keel on a yacht. But a yacht can set sail. The immobility of bricks and mortar made you vulnerable, especially if dark forces got wind of your address. Right now,

Lennie thought, if they lived in the Firefly they'd have the strategic option of rapid movement for both offence and defence, plus easy camouflage by way of spray paint and flipping rego number plates. But *c'est la vie*, as Aunty D used to say. Nothing for it but to defend the castle!

It was winter, so dusk was arriving early, providing handy cover for the body transfers and ride across the city to the Galaxy Motel.

7 - LOVECRAFT

IN THE BACK GARDEN, the headlights of the Firefly glowed in the laneway above the picket fence. Lennie stepped to the gate and unbolted the latch. Joe parked with the van's sliding side-door next to the gate. They moved with pace to the shed.

"Well, look at you!" said Joe, smiling at Tremlett who appeared to be in love with the chair. "Happy as a pig in a party hat."

Tremlett was peering at the rusty, corrugated iron ceiling, his eyes travelling about as if he was exploring a wonderful scene.

"Are we in the desert?" said Tremlett, gazing at an ochre-coloured stain surrounded by dark specks. "It's a beautiful land-scape. Those eagles are fantastic, aren't they?...is that Uluru I can see?...course, it's really Ayres Rock, not that abo name...don't you hate that political correctness crap?...if it wasn't for a white man, that fucking place wouldn't be on the map!"

"Yes, Ronnie. It's Uluru you can see," said Lennie, who was even more convinced of his business idea to slip laughing gas into movie theatres and other entertainment venues. And what about shopping centres, he thought? When the salesgirl said, "You look ten years younger in those skinny jeans, Mr Bigbottom," the clothes would simply walk off the rack.

While Tremlett and Lennie discussed the joys of outback tourism, Joe injected Ketamine into a vein on top of Tremlett's hand, whose body went floppy pretty quickly. But his eyes remained alight.

Lennie said, "Your ambulance is here now, Ronnie."

"Oh, yeah. Ambo," said Tremlett, his eyeballs rolling. "I'm nod veeling doo vell."

Joe believed he'd put enough Ketamine into Tremlett to knock out one of the horses it was usually injected into before surgery. But Tremlett's consciousness was as stubborn as a beetroot stain on a white shirt. The detective seemed to be a regular user of strong drugs and had serious tolerance. This was one of the advantages of being in the police force, thought Joe: you get more free drugs than old-aged pensioners.

They hauled Tremlett off the chair and held him under the armpits.

Tremlett mumbled happily, "Hup, two, three, four," over and over, as if he was a marching soldier. The three men stumbled towards the back gate.

"Not ambo," Tremlett said as Joe hurled open the side door of the van.

"It's a special one," said Lennie. "VIP service just for you, Ronnie."

They sat Tremlett on the floor inside the Firefly's open door, leaving his feet resting on the tar outside. Tremlett's glassy eyes looked up at Joe, "Is that you, Downy boy? Mr Ranga Downs? Koo-koo-koo! Ka-ka-ka!"

Tremlett laughed again like a kookaburra.

Joe usually liked being compared with orangutans. He looked up and down the lane. No witnesses. He dialled his favourite weapon to stun, not kill – and drove his fist into Tremlett's nose, short and sharp. Tremlett reeled and fell on his back into the van, silent. Joe flicked Tremlett's legs in, then turned to rejoin Lennie in the garden.

As they stacked the shoveler, the last of the three, into the van, TC appeared. "Found the car," he said. "There must be good money in thieving off thieves. It's a Range Rover Sports. Latest model. It'd cost circa, a hundred and fifty thousand dollars, maybe more."

"Tremlett's dumber than he looks," said Lennie, "if he tools around town flashing that sort of rig."

"I don't think it's his. I think it's hers. It's painted gold. And the rego plates are pink. First letters, N-C-Y. There was a GoPro camera on the dash, but I ripped it out."

Lennie smiled at the image of Nancy's car. It fitted in with his grand plan in an odd way. "Joe, can you put some pink lippy on and drive the bling-mobile? TC and I will spin around in the Firefly and meet you in the street."

"Aren't we forgetting something?" said Joe, deciding to ignore Lennie's fashion advice.

"What?"

"*Our* bling."

"Ay caramba!" said Lennie, slapping his forehead. "TC, keep an eye on this lot, will you? We'll be back in a sec...by the way, have you got a decent camera phone?"

TC nodded. "What if they wake up?"

"Massage their minds with that," said Lennie, pointing at a greened bronze statue of a squid-headed monster with dragon's wings that sat in a garden bed by the gate.

"Hit them with it?" said TC, ogling the football-sized beast.

"Up to you," said Lennie. "But the last bloke we showed it to shit himself simply at the sight of it."

TC narrowed his eyes in thought. "HP Lovecraft. Am I right?"

"Like a bit of cosmic horror, do you, TC?" said Lennie. "I found that thing in a junk shop along with one of his books. Gift set."

Joe shook his head. Lennie had named his air-powered spear-gun after the dead American author. To Joe, the guy sounded like a peddler of sex toys or a carpenter who enjoyed belting nails. If Joe had his way, the sea monster would disappear over the back fence, probably up the lane into the garden of Father Bernardo, an occasional public nudist who resided in the local Catholic Church where there were much creepier things than statues, as he and Lennie learned as kids.

Joe clarified for TC. "The bloke who flipped his lid over Mr Squidly there was dosed to the gills with magic mushrooms, so he had a flying start. Anyway, let's crack on here, hey?"

TC tried to lift the green monster but failed to get it off the ground.

Lennie and Joe went into the house where Joe opened the door to a closet under the staircase. He pulled out an uninflated, blow-up rubber doll made in the image of an adult woman; a pair of mirrored aviator-style sunglasses; and plucked from a hook on the back of the door several chunky, gold-chain necklaces, plus a blue velvet drawstring bag whose insides tinkled when he shook it.

"Yeah," said Lennie. "Nice touch...I'll grab my laptop."

"And the Ket-kit," called Joe. "And here, don't forget your hat."

Joe reached into the closet and tossed Lennie a floppy cloth hat which had wavy brown hair cascading from its inner headband.

"We better take this too," said Joe, lifting a shoebox from a shelf. He opened the lid and checked that it contained a face-painting kit with brushes and pots of many colours.

"Jesus," said Lennie, stroking his shaven pate and putting the hat on, the glued-in locks caressing his shoulders. "It's like going on holiday. I'll grab a backpack."

8 - GALAXY MOTEL

THE GALAXY MOTEL'S entrance was signposted by a neon-yellow ball the size of a small car that was skewered upon a tomato-red pole. A violet ring hula-hooped around the ball.

Further down the pole, the word *Vacancy* glowed in orange letters inside a white lightbox.

Joe cruised slowly past the signpost in the Range Rover and didn't turn into the driveway. Best to sniff before you bite, he reminded himself.

Joe might have been a dunderhead at school as his head-master, Mr Darian, informed him most days after classes. And Darian had given Joe the same assessment on the more recent night of the gob-smacked teacher's unexpected encounter with a bronze squid statue. But Joe was smart enough to know that the suburb of Lakemba in south-western Sydney was more famous for its mosques and halal butchers than its themed motels. Apart from the pretty entrance, why had Lennie chosen this joint for this evening's show, he wondered?

He circled the block. Men wearing long beards and bowl-shaped prayer hats paraded across the footpath as Joe waited to enter the Galaxy's driveway. From their looks, Joe got the impression they weren't keen on blokes driving gold cars with pink number plates. Mavis sat shiny and still as stone in the seat beside him, looking straight ahead.

He phoned Lennie. "I feel like a fish out of water."

"You'll be back in the wet shortly, mate," said Lennie, sensitive to Joe's occasional belief that he was a humpback whale trapped in a human body. "I'll call you on approach."

Joe motored under a roofed area beside the glass-walled reception office and stopped. He turned to his passenger. "Keep your seatbelt on, Mavis, while I pop inside and get us a room."

Joe checked in the rearview mirror to make sure that all of his red hair was tucked inside his black beanie. After adjusting his mirrored sunnies, he tinkered with several chunky, plastic-gold chains that hung around his neck and draped to his belly button. His long-sleeved purple T-shirt, black jeans, and new white training shoes were the best he could come up with at short notice. He opened the blue velvet drawstring bag that he'd brought from home and plucked out a gold-banded ring that displayed a ruby sapphire as big as a dove's egg.

He popped the party-shop jewel on a middle finger and looked through the windscreen toward the motel's office, then scanned the outer walls. It didn't look like the place had CCTV. Joe started to like the Galaxy Motel.

*

A few blocks away, Lennie parked the Firefly kerbside to an empty sports field in shadows under a large tree. He turned to TC. "Mate, I need you to play lookout while I make adjustments to the van. Best you jump out and scan the street. You can whistle, can't you?"

TC did one of those eardrum-ripping, two-fingers-in-the-mouth toots that Lennie had never been able to master, and opened his door, sliding out feet first. It took a while for the soles of his tasseled shoes to hit the ground.

Lennie ducked under Rawcus's riding rod between the seat headrests, careful not to dislodge his floppy hat-and-hair combo. He clambered over the snoring passengers, glad he was wearing boots because a few teeth protruded from lips that looked as hygienic as the Komodo dragon's choppers he'd seen at the zoo last week.

Opening a wall cabinet, he extracted two car number plates, plus a battery-powered drill into which he inserted a bit for driving and un-driving screws.

He lifted grey, zip-front overalls off a wall hook, and climbed into them. From a shelf beside the cabinet, he collected several rolls of magnetic sheeting that matched the off-white external paintwork of the van.

Outside, Lennie worked as slickly as a racetrack pitman switching the phantom numberplates onto the van. He unfurled the blank magnetic sheets and began sticking them on the sides of the Firefly. The words *Fire Alarms, Home Security, Video Surveillance, Broadband, TV and Audio, General Electrical* disappeared, along with the company name, *Firefly Electrics*.

Night had arrived with its full black cloak. Lennie signalled for TC to get back in the van. Climbing behind the steering wheel, Lennie reached into a door pocket from which he extracted a pair of black-framed spectacles that had zero optical quality. He put them on.

TC shook his head. "What if we get busted by the honest police?"

"We'll plead insanity."

*

Lennie phoned Joe.

Joe said, "I'm in the room with Mavis...Yeah, two double beds. I paid cash. The bloke didn't blink. Whacked it straight into his pocket...Well, he did look over his counter through the window at Mavis and gave me a wink."

Lennie chortled. "Told you the Galaxy was the right place for this. Can I back up to the door, though?"

"Could be tricky."

*

Lennie drove slowly along the main road so as not to attract the attention of the law, or blow the masking-sheets off the Firefly. He took a bend. Something clunked in the back of the van, followed by a dull click. Lennie glanced over his shoulder; the shoveler had rolled off his stacked companions and slammed his shoulder into a door near the handle. Had he opened it?

"Crosswalk!" cried TC.

Lennie spun back to face-forward and slammed the brakes. "Shit!"

The nose of the van was poking onto a zebra crossing – over which a boy and a dog on a lead were walking. The boy showed Lennie his middle finger. Lennie waved apologetically.

"Uh-oh," said TC, looking into his rearview mirror.

Whoop-whoop!

Lennie's wing mirror reflected a blue-and-white checkerboard band around a stocky sedan car that bristled with antennas. The police car flashed its headlights.

"Quick," Lennie said. "There's a painter's drop sheet behind your seat. Throw it over those fuckers. And yourself."

"They stink," said TC.

"If our insanity plea fails, there'll be a conga line in your cell that stinks worse."

TC scurried into the back and disappeared under the canvas.

Lennie pulled over to the kerb near a bus stop on a street bustling with pedestrians and traffic. Hanging by a bootlace from the rearview mirror, there was a little-finger-shaped piece of Bloodwood tree. Lennie touched the Jack.

He stayed seat-belted and left the motor running as the police car parked behind him. If this goes pear-shaped, he thought, I'll whack the Firefly into reverse and smash their engine. Cop car motors are specially engineered for king-hits, but I might at least pop their airbags and shock the shit of them while I hit the accelerator. It was an iffy plan, he concluded, but it was the best he had.

"Hang on to something, TC. This could get bumpy. You might need to swing that door open and roll our buddies out along the way."

"What?" squeaked TC.

"Shush," whispered Lennie. "We have company." He rolled down his window.

"You've broken the law," the policeman said.

"How so, officer?"

"Running a crosswalk with a pedestrian on it."

"Ah, I believe I nudged the law, but didn't break it," said Lennie. "I didn't actually cross the line."

"So your name is Mr Smartarse, is it?"

Lennie smiled.

The officer took a flashlight off his belt. He leaned close to Lennie's face to shine the torch around the front cabin, so close that Lennie felt the young man's warm breath on his skin. As the officer moved the beam over Lennie's shoulder to probe the back, Lennie smelled something familiar. No, not cigarettes. He looked into the man's glassy eyes, at his wide black pupils and too-pink whites. Fuck me, thought Lennie, this cheeky bastard has been on the bong. I should know. And there was something else on his breath, a smell like paint thinners. Crystal meth? Maybe a weed and ice cocktail? Whatever it was had been consumed not too long ago. Maybe minutes, and possibly in the patrol car.

"I can smell smoke," said Lennie. "Did you get a whiff of that, officer?"

"What?"

"It smells like marijuana, and some other chemical. That stuff's illegal, isn't it? Maybe it's coming from this halal butcher's shop next to us. Muslims, they smoke hashish, don't they?"

"Sir. I don't think...," The officer's voice trailed away, his eyelids fluttered; he clutched a hand to his chest as if his heart was doing something odd and he needed to get a grip on it.

"You alright, officer? You don't look well."

A bus beeped its horn behind them. Cheeky coppers, cheeky bus drivers. This was a strange part of the city, thought Lennie, returning the grins of two men smoking a twin-hosed hooker pipe and drinking coffee at a table on the pavement outside a barber's shop next door to a kebab house. Maybe he should come here for a head-shave and lunch with Joe. Just not with bodies in the back of the Firefly. The drivers of the cars behind the waiting bus started blowing their horns, apparently oblivious, or unconcerned, that a cop car was holding up the show.

Lennie lifted the frame of his spectacles off his nose as if to expand his nasal cavities. He made a few deep sniffing sounds, like a hound onto a scent, and said, "If there's nothing else officer, I'll be off. We shouldn't hold up our fellow citizens who are trying to get home after a hard day on the tools, should we?"

"Sure. Sure," said the sweaty-browed officer, putting a finger to his jugular vein to test his pulse as he stepped back, blinking as if he was seeing things that he'd rather not.

Lennie knew the signs of a panic attack well enough. He'd had plenty. But he'd learned to ride them like they were bare-backed ponies. Smoking dope mostly made them buck harder. It was an even wilder ride with meth, as he'd discovered in jail, which was why he avoided it on the outside. This baby-faced copper looked like he was new to the sport; he staggered back to his car.

The patrol car did a U-turn and skedaddled. Lennie drove up the road and turned into the driveway of the Galaxy Motel.

TC poked his little head from under the drop sheet and chimed, "Are we there yet?"

9 - HONEY

LENNIE ROLLED the nameless van past the Galaxy's reception office, comforted that no staff or guests were visible inside. He idled beside a fence and mentally noted how well-configured the motel was for their purposes.

The block of land, after you passed the hula-hooped planet, was a long-sided rectangle that housed a row of 20 rooms with an angled parking spot in front of each unit.

Beyond Room 20, there was a wavy picket fence, and beyond that, a wide street leading into the suburban labyrinth of Lakemba. Lennie concluded that if the shit hit the fan, the van, which had a steel cattle-bar protecting its nose, would make woodchips of the rickety fence. Hopefully.

Pauline had tipped Lennie off about the Galaxy months ago. Not because she was a gypsy with a crystal ball about today's events, although she did dabble in clairvoyance via a ouija board. She'd chanced upon the place while collecting a mother and three kids who were hiding there, before taking them to the refuge that she managed in another part of the city. Pauline reckoned Lennie would love the 1950s-era, sci-fi signs out the front and showed him pictures. Lennie had later taken a solo gander while Joe was out of town.

Now, Lennie watched Joe climb into the gold car parked outside Room 13. He re-parked in an unoccupied bay outside Room 14.

Lennie drove the van forward past bay 13. He reversed into the parking space until the back tyres were stopped by the concrete edge of the veranda floor. He and TC climbed out to assess. Joe joined them.

There was still more than a body's length gap between the motel room's door and the van's double back doors. Alien voices murmured.

Lennie cocked an ear toward the van. "Is that Tremlett speaking in tongues?"

"Wrong direction," said Joe, turning to face the door to Room 12. It opened.

A round woman, dressed in a chocolate-brown dress hemmed with gold braid and a matching headscarf, held the hand of a rake-thin man wearing a grey suit and white kaftan shirt. He sported a long grey beard. A white prayer hat sat upon his skull. The elderly couple stepped onto the veranda.

"Good evening," said Lennie with a courteous nod.

The couple smiled politely and strolled towards a sparkling white sedan parked in front of their room.

"Looks like you are dressed for an important event," Lennie continued. "Something special?"

"My niece's wedding party," said the woman.

"I trust there's a long and enjoyable night ahead of you then. Our best wishes to your family."

"Thank you."

As the couple drove away, the trio from Room 13 waved.

TC said, "You are quite sneaky, Lennie."

"Just gathering intel. And I do hope they have a nice *long* night. These walls look thin."

"No. I mean your hat," said TC. "The built-in hair."

"Made it myself. Arts and crafts are very therapeutic. You just need a wig, an old hat, some glue..."

Joe cupped a hand over his mouth. "Incoming," he whispered.

A handful of motel guests with stern faces walked with purpose behind the parked vehicles, heading for the street. Thumping erupted inside the van. The passers-by paused.

"A dog," Joe explained to the furrow-browed mob, who turned their attention to Joe's ruby ring and gold chains. "Rotty just needs a feed."

The guests hastened way, apparently fearful of being fed to a Rottweiler.

Lennie said, "We need to shove these bodies into the room fast, otherwise the cops will be getting calls about an unlicensed morgue."

Joe said, "Let's bounce the Firefly onto the veranda. As long as we don't treat 'em like chooks eggs, it'll take a few seconds to drag these dozy pricks straight in. I'll drive."

Lennie and TC stepped into Room 13 and put on surgical gloves. TC began tugging the room's night curtains across the veranda windows. Lennie stood in the open doorway to guide Joe in.

Joe motored forward a little to give himself a run-up. He slipped the gearshift into reverse and hit the accelerator, jumping the back tyres over the veranda's edge. He braked, but the red-painted surface was slippery. Thunk! The wall stopped him. He drove forward a tad.

Lennie pulled open the Firefly's rear doors – and waved Joe back towards him until the door's edges were almost touching the motel's wall. Joe stayed at the wheel, engine idling, his eyes peeled for witnesses.

Lennie dragged the shoveller out by the feet, clunking his head on the floor which was carpeted with faded planets and stars and rocket ships. The concrete slab under the worn carpet was less kind to the fatter heads of big-hardhat and Nancy, who groaned unhelpfully loudly as they hit the floor.

Lennie, pleased their thick-skinned guests had not split their heads and started trickling evidence, grabbed his backpack from the rear of the Firefly and threw its doors shut.

Joe parked neatly in bay 13, locked the van, and joined the others inside the room, bolting the security chain.

The three bodies lay side-by-side on the floor, limbs restrained by gaffer tape. Nancy was on her back, blinking into the flickering tube of a fluorescent ceiling light. The shoveller was on his side, snoring with a whistling sound. Tremlett faced the carpet, mumbling about "comets" and "monsters".

"Medicine time," said Joe. "Mr Tremlett, in particular, seems to have a tolerance to Ket."

"Too right," said Lennie, who placed his backpack on a wall-side bench and pulled out the sunglasses case which he opened. It contained a pink rubber band, a short pencil, a fresh bottle of Ketamine, and two disposable syringes.

He held up the syringes. Lennie didn't like needles; they made him think about his recent diagnosis with a new strain of potentially fatal liver virus called hepatitis G, which his specialist doctor concluded he must have picked up in prison and for which there was no cure yet.

Lennie said, "They're extortionist pricks, and probably worse, but possibly spreading a nasty virus between them won't help us sleep at night."

Joe said, "OK. No sharing. By mouth for Nancy, then. The boy galahs have better veins anyway."

Joe arranged the medicine kit on the bathroom vanity.

In the main room, Lennie and TC set up the laptop on a two-seater dining table beside a wall. As well as twin double beds, the main room contained a kitchenette, a wall-mounted TV, and built-in wardrobes.

"Joe," TC called. "Did you get a password for the motel Wi-Fi?"

"Yep," said Joe, stepping out of the bathroom with a half-full syringe. "It's with the room receipt on top of the fridge."

Joe dragged the rubber band over Tremlett's wrist, stuck the pencil inside the band, and twisted until the veins on top of his hand bulged. He swabbed the skin with an alcohol wipe and injected the plumpest vein.

TC tapped the laptop keyboard. "Lennie, I need those clean memory sticks."

Lennie reached into his backpack and tossed TC the data sticks. "Joe and I will dress the set."

*

Joe tossed into a corner of the room three pairs of undies which joined a pile of lemon-fluoro safety vests, shirts, pants, work boots, and a bra. He iced the pile with a spandex belly-flattener that had sprung from the porridge torso of DS Ronnie Tremlett.

"What do you think, Mavis?" Joe said to the black-haired, blow-up doll who was standing and leaning against the curtained windows. Mavis appeared to be eyeing the bed in front of her. Joe asked, "Want to play stacks on the mill too? No? I don't blame you. You're just here to watch."

TC tapped the keyboard without looking up. "Voyeurism is the word you're after, Joe."

"You're the expert," said Joe. "I saw that telescope in your bedroom."

"Oh. That's for stargazing."

"It had a landscape lens."

TC blushed.

"Showtime," said Lennie, standing in front of the bed upon which Tremlett & Co. were stacked in a sweaty heap.

Tremlett was bum-down on the mattress; the back of his skull, neck, and hairy shoulders were propped against the head-board; his plump pink legs were spread. All he was wearing were black socks. Planted in his lap was the face of his similarly-clothed brother-in-law.

TC began viewing the scene through the high-definition camera on his phone, scampering about like a Hollywood lens-man checking the angles and the lighting.

"This arrangement will be alright for still shots," TC said of Lennie's and Joe's set. "But we will need movement for the video.

And their eyes are closed. Of course, that might be perceived by the viewer as pleasure-induced. But it'd be better to have them open."

"Mm," said Joe, who began opening and closing kitchen cupboards near the fridge and sink. "Ah-ha," he said, rifling through a straw basket containing tea bags, coffee sachets, and sugar packets. "Honey."

"And your idea is?" said TC.

10 - SHOWTIME

JOE OPENED a single-serve container and stuck the pad of an index finger into the amber goo.

He stepped over to Tremlett and smeared the sticky stuff over one of the detective's closed upper eyelids. He tried to pinch Tremlett's eyelash between his thumb and index finger. But Joe might as well have used a pair of baseball bats as chopsticks for eating noodles.

He huffed. "TC, do you mind?"

TC protested. "You know I have obsessive-repulsive-disorder."

Lennie cocked an eye at TC. "I thought your OCD only applied to cleaning kitchens and bathrooms."

"You're not listening to me," said TC. "I said, *repulsive* disorder. I can't stand touching people's eyes."

"Oh, for fuck's sake," said Lennie. "I'll do it."

Lennie pinched Tremlett's upper eyelash and dragged the lid up, gluing the skin to the flesh under his eyebrow. He figured the Ketamine's muscle-relaxing powers should have weakened both Tremlett's ability, and his want, to close his eyes, even when his retina's got hit by the room lights. He was right.

Lennie honeyed the other eyelid and stuck it open.

"Ooh," said Joe. "He looks like he can see us, but he can't, all at once."

Tremlett's tongue drooped from his mouth.

"Excellent," said TC, taking a sample shot. "Creepy as."

"This phony fucker gets phonier all the time," said Lennie, looking at the patch of skin below Tremlett's left eye. "It's a fake, fake tear."

"That's what you call a tongue-twister," said TC, studying Tremlett's screen test.

Lennie wiped Tremlett's teardrop tattoo with a tissue; it left nothing but a blue tinge on the skin of the cheekbone.

Lennie looked at the floor, pondering. "Ronnie likes to wear make-up to cover up who he really is, right? Well, he's the star of this show. The focus of our production is what *he* is doing. Not so much *who* he is doing it with. Am I wrong?"

Joe and TC looked at each other and shook their heads as if in mutual agreement that Lennie was now aboard one of the rocket ships he was eyeing on the carpet.

Lennie looked up. "Joe, the face paint. I think we can do Nancy and Shovel-boy here a small favour. A bit of identity blurring might be in order for the secondary players. Especially if they land on the internet in front of a global audience. These experiences can scar for life."

"Fair enough," said Joe, who opened the box of face paints. "Animals?"

"Ooh, there's a twist," said TC. "Bestiality."

Joe smothered Nancy's face in Prussian blue, capping her nose with black, and streaking her cheeks three white lines aside.

"Meow!" said TC, scratching the air with his fingers. "I really enjoyed the musical, hated the movie. Andrew Lloyd Webber called the film ridiculous. What about you guys?"

Lennie shook his head. "Can you stay focussed?"

Joe trowled the shoveler's face with grey, put white upon his ears, and blackened his nose.

"Koala?" guessed Lennie, recalling the sight of a naked man who had recently accosted him and Joe in a city street and clung to a tree trunk, asking for a back rub and insisting he was a bush bear, not a madman. Lennie had recently jotted this experience into a notebook, joining it to other memorable encounters of recent years.

"Oh, dear," said TC. "Our detective appears to have lost interest in the acting business."

They turned to Tremlett. His eyes had come unstuck and were closed.

TC said, "You guys have any superglue in your van?"

"Might blind him," said Lennie.

TC arched his brow. "That'd reduce his chances of a return visit to your home. And he'd have trouble ID'ing you in a court of law."

"True," Lennie replied, "but he's not that high on our Colour Scheme, is he, Joe?"

"He'll get Red if Rawcus dies," answered Joe, who was reading a text message that Mrs G had just sent him about Rawcus's condition...

*

The Colour Scheme by which Lennie and Joe rated the characters they encountered in life was born while they sailed upon a glassy green sea aboard their little yacht, *Flamingo Sky*.

Lennie had been leaning against the mainmast with the rigging clanking on the rise and fall of a gentle swell. Joe had been lying naked and face-up on a towel on the rear deck, admiring clouds that made him think of mashed-potato lambs.

Lennie had said, "You know, mate, people cook up – and keep – all sorts of nastiness in their heads. There's no stopping that, and nor should there be.

"But when you let it spill out through your hands and feet – or you shoot your mouth off in a vicious way – well, things change. Borders are crossed. People deliver hurt, and people get hurt."

"Uh, huh," Joe had said, fearing Lennie was drifting into space that only Lennie could understand.

"There should be consequences when you deliberately hurt someone who's done you no harm. Know what I mean?"

Joe's heart galloped; the clouds were turning from fluffy lambs into the darkly-furrowed face of a man with huge nostrils and hairy hands that were reaching from the heavens for Joe's body.

Joe jumped up. "Give me a sec," he said, kneeling by a gunwale. He cupped a hand and scooped it over the side, filling it with water which he splashed on his face trying to wash away the vision of his old headmaster, Mr Darian. Joe tucked the towel around his waist. "OK, I'm good."

"I'm talking here about failures in the system," Lennie continued, "where people literally get away with murder, and the like."

"Go on," said Joe, who glanced overhead, relieved that the fluffy lambs were returning.

"We need a rating system."

"Got something in mind?"

Lennie gazed at the shimmering horizon. "There are seven key colours in the rainbow, right? An odd number, which is important." He used his fingers to count them off: "Red, orange, yellow, green, blue, indigo, and violet."

"I think I'm getting it," said Joe. "Your gran's name was Violet."

Lennie flashed a thumbs-up. "I reckon that's it. Father Francesco would be a red, same as Darian. And everyone else is in between."

Lennie's faith in the odd-numbered, rainbow-coloured, rating system of human character was reinforced when he realised that no matter how small, or big, an odd number gets, if you shove a fulcrum under the middle number, the whole lot balances perfectly all the way to both ends of infinity. That was a scale of justice he could grasp.

Back at home the night after their day sailing, Lennie had dug a book from the shelf in the sitting room and read a quote to Joe: "*I think there are certain crimes which the law cannot touch, and which, therefore, to some extent, justify private revenge. Sherlock Holmes, The Adventure of Charles Augustus Milverton.*"

"Now," said Lennie. "Holmes was a pommy tosser, but he had a point. We're just sharpening it."

Lennie and Joe retired that evening after agreeing that if someone was an absolute prick who got away with murder or monstering a child or the like, such as Francesco and Darian, they got a red sticker. Orange and yellow were grades for lesser evils.

Green was neutral turf, but those people would come up for regular review.

Blues, indigos, and violets were indicators for top-shelf characters like Pauline Gerrity and, if they needed it, they received support, like cash, or being taken to the shops, or having their faulty washing machine and lights fixed for free.

Categorising people, of course, was a tricky task. In the end, it boiled down to "available evidence", and Lennie and Joe had different methods for obtaining evidence than did the cops or so-called Courts of Law administered by the State.

Under their system, there was no *Get Out of Jail Free* card like there was in the regular system that Sherlock Holmes also had a problem with, a system where a villain's lawyer could say stuff like "you didn't get that evidence the right way" and the case gets thrown out of court, even though it's clear the guy tossed petrol on his girlfriend and set her on fire.

Lennie and Joe dubbed their system *F for Ethics,* and it evolved over ensuing months. But it was not smooth sailing. For if Lennie rated someone by any colour at all, Joe would have a chance to argue the toss, and vice versa. Pauline was consulted on projects related to her women's refuge.

In the time they'd been operating *F for Ethics*, Lennie and Joe had never reached a stalemate, which was handy because they didn't have a clear resolution mechanism if they disagreed.

They'd thought about bringing Rawcus in and putting food dye on a couple of pumpkin seeds – one representing Lennie's selected colour and the other Joe's – and letting the bird choose the final colour. And they'd thought about a coin toss. But they concluded that both approaches were a tad casual, especially if red was involved. So they just argued for however long it took to reach an agreement.

*

"Perfecto!" declared TC, who was doing final screen tests for the freshly made-up characters in Room 13. "Nice job on Ronnie's eyes, Lennie. Truly innovative."

"Cheers," said Lennie, packing a pair of surgical scissors and a box of flesh-coloured sticking plasters back into the first-aid kit from the Firefly. After washing Tremlett's honeyed eyelids clean using alcohol swabs, and drying them with a hairdryer from the motel bathroom, he had snipped the glue-ends off a couple of plasters and rolled them sticky-side-out around a pencil. The resulting tubes held Tremlett's eyes open by adhering his top eyelids to the skin of his under-brow.

TC sucked his lips with concentration. "Look, this is great for a few still shots. But we'll need some dynamism for the video. The viewing public won't buy the show without it."

"Dynamism?" said Joe, who'd heard of the word but hadn't yet given the world of *isms* a deep dig in his adult literacy class.

"Movement," TC explained. "Jiggy-jiggy."

Joe grinned and lay on the floor, trying to stay out of camera view. He jiggled the bedframe with his hands as if he was weight-lifting his cut-down railway tracks in the garden at home.

"Huzza!" cried TC, showing a thumbs-up. He tapped *record* on his phone.

Lennie called, "Take one. Scene one. *The Beasts of Burden.*"

The filmmakers spent about half an hour moving their three, uncomplaining actors through a range of amorous positions.

Lennie said, "OK. Time for the climax."

He and Joe arranged Tremlett in the bed flat on his back with his glazed eyes staring straight into TC's lens. They placed the cat woman stomach-to-stomach on top of the detective and stacked the koala man stomach down on her back. Mavis leaned against the curtains watching, her mouth open, as always, as if shocked at what she was witnessing. The bodies bounced. One of Tremlett's eyelids fell to half-closed above the blue smudge of the blurred teardrop.

"Oh, this is very moody," said TC, zooming in on the shifty eye before going back to a wide shot. "Nice."

TC hit pause. "Joe, can you move to the foot of the bed and vary the speeds for the home straight?"

"Jesus, mate," Joe groaned, sliding along the carpet. "This isn't the Melbourne Cup." He used both hands to lift the bed, working it up and down, trying not to topple the sweaty stack. He glanced into a wall mirror. The shoveler was sliding off Nancy's back.

"Whoopsie," Joe said, as the man thudded headfirst to the floor.

"Let's take a break," said Lennie. "I've had an idea. Give me a few minutes, will you?"

He left the room.

He returned with a bottle inside a brown paper bag and something hidden inside the belly of his T-shirt. From the bag, he extracted a tall bottle of sweet Sambuca, and from his shirt a plastic sandwich bag of Mars Grass.

"Bit early to party, mate," said Joe.

"I hate Sambuca," said TC.

Lennie shook his head. "It's not for us."

Lennie opened the Sambuca and splashed every drop of the sticky aniseed spirit over the pile of stirring but still compliant humans, arranging Tremlett's hand to clasp the empty bottle's neck and tuck it by his side.

TC took a few more shots, then set to work editing the video on Lennie's laptop at the table.

Joe pulled the air-plug from Mavis's belly button. "It'd get ugly if someone dropped a match on them right now," he said, squeezing Mavis flat by starting with her feet as if doing reflexology. "Remember what happened in that pizza joint?"

"Scarred me for life," said Lennie, tapping his skull. How could he forget the eye-popping sight of a glass of Sambuca being tossed through the burning wicks of a candelabra on a table in an Italian restaurant, whereupon the airborne liqueur burst into flames as blue as kerosene and grilled the face, chest, and hands of a man who'd upset his dining companion?

"You're not gonna do it here, are you?" said Joe.

"Tempting," said Lennie, who sat at the table beside TC and watched him editing.

Lennie checked that his surgical gloves were still well-fitted and started rolling a joint of Mars Grass with cigarette papers.

He felt a tickle, an unscratchable itch erupting inside his skull. He closed his eyes and saw purple sparks in the dark. The sparks coalesced, turned into yapping dogs, trying to break their chains, desperate to burst from the black into the light, thrusting to break into the physical world. Lennie felt the dogs running inside his hands, biting his nerves, making his fingers twitch. Did he quite literally want to *cook* these shifty characters in Room 13? He took a Zippo lighter from an overalls pocket and flipped the lid open, and closed it, and open...

Lennie looked up at the yellowing smoke detector on the ceiling. No, he thought, they sure as hell didn't need the fire brigade being called right now. But after studying the detector, him being an electrician with experience in these matters, he decided it was a good bet that the motel's owner was a cheap-arse who squibbed on maintenance. So, if there was smoke in the room, the fire alarm would most likely be useless. He stepped to the kitchenette sink and dabbed his gloved index finger into a dripping tap spout. He wetted the gum on the rollie paper and finished the joint. He tossed the Zippo to Joe.

Lennie made a loose fist with a gloved hand and tucked the reefer between the upper bones of his middle fingers so that it stuck up like a smokestack. He blocked the far end of this fist with the other palm and sucked through a hole he created by circling his thumb and index finger. Joe fired the Zippo's flame and held it to the tip of the joint.

"Why the fancy rig?" Joe inquired.

"DNA," said Lennie, puffing smoke.

Lennie had a few more puffs, took the joint over to Tremlett's mouth and shoved it between the copper's lips, giving it a decent wipe around to get plenty of drool on the cigarette paper. He stubbed it out in a saucer on the bedside table and left it there.

"What a day," said Lennie, who started sprinkling crumbs of fresh Mars Grass on the floor.

He kicked a couple of buds under the bed. He figured that when they woke, if Tremlett & Co wanted to call the cops – bent ones, or straight ones – they could explain the weed, the near-empty bottle of horse tranquiliser in the fridge, the needle marks on their hands, and the syringes which had been wrapped in toilet paper and planted in the bathroom bin. But moreover, Lennie hoped that by leaving these props lying around, it would reinforce to a waking Tremlett the sort of tricky possibilities that lay ahead of him, should he wish to pursue a vendetta.

TC lifted his gaze from the laptop screen. "Want to review the production?"

Lennie and Joe stood behind TC as he kicked off with highlights of the motel party. He'd signed off with Tremlett's dentist chair confession about his criminal conspiracy in the company of his brother-in-law and Nancy Enoka. TC had pixelated any images of Lennie and Joe and disguised their voices.

"One last job, Spielberg," said Lennie. He passed TC a motel pen and pad. "They say I write like a doctor, and Joe's still at school."

"What if they trace me?"

"These people don't even know you exist," said Lennie. "You may not have noticed but they've been out like lights since you entered stage left."

"You know I'm ambidextrous," said TC. "I guess I could go off-piste and use my non-preferred."

"Use your feet if you like, but crack on. The bastards are stirring and we're out of Ket."

TC began writing a note dictated by Lennie with advice from Joe.

Dear Mr Tremlett and friends,

Please find attached a memory stick to help you recall your adventures today.

Feel free to keep it, or have copies made for each of you. We have made plenty for ourselves.

In fact, if you try to pull your Sydney Water worker stunt again, or anything like it, copies of your home movie will be sent to every TV and newspaper outlet, social media platform (ie global), politician, and police station in the city. They will also be placed in the interstate post for delivery across borders. In the entertainment industry, this is described as a general release. You may have heard the term. It would make good comedy on porn sites too.

Alternatively, you can have a shower, get dressed, and fuck off into the filth and darkness from where you came. Your car is waiting for you out front.

If you take the latter and intelligent course, we will keep your memories in a safe place, pending your long-term good behaviour. Life?

Au revoir.

PS: It appears that in Lakemba motels, they keep copies of the holy Koran in the rooms, as opposed to the once Christian monopoly of the New Testament (Gideon's Bible is a name that springs to mind). Anyway, as you will see in your movie, you three did some very unholy things with that Koran. And you had all that toilet tissue in the bathroom. Tut, tut. The important point is, we have made a director's cut of this part of your escapade, with a close up of your badge, Detective Sergeant Tremlett (and a copy of your home address via your driver's licence which was in your wallet), that will go to every mosque in town, if we ever see your shadows in our lives again.

*

Thunder rocked the city. Under spitting rain and blistering light, Joe placed folded Mavis in the back of the Firefly. Lennie sat in the front passenger seat, TC stood in the gap between the seats.

Joe climbed behind the wheel.

TC said, "Why does Joe always drive?"

"I drive," Lennie protested.

"Not when Joe's around."

"I've got a disease," Lennie conceded.

TC reeled back. "Disease?"

"Every time I grab the steering wheel I get a powerful urge to engage enthusiastically with people who drive like me."

"Huh?"

"He's wanking on," said Joe. "Normal people call it road rage."

TC relaxed. "There's a treatment for that, I'm sure."

"I'm onto it," said Lennie, who took three cans of beer from the cooler by his feet, snapped the tops, and passed them around. Lennie dragged the cooler into the floor space between the seats and patted its top. He nodded at TC. "Why don't you sit here?"

TC perched atop the cooler clutching a beer. As the Firefly left the Galaxy, he swung his spare hand above his head and gripped Rawcus's rod like a monkey bar.

Lennie, his eyes fixed upon the windscreen, reached down and ruffled TC's hair. "Hang in there, comrade."

Unlike TC, Joe knew that Lennie was actually talking to himself.

"You OK?" said Joe.

"Just trying to see off my visitors," replied Lennie, who was peering at the rain through the windscreen.

Joe had never met Lennie's visitors, not in person. The doctors called them delusions or illusions and other fancy words. Whatever they were, they came and went. And so Lennie and Joe had decided to entertain them without calling for external help. These visitors rarely stayed more than a few hours at a time, and over the years they had proved to be less trouble than the adults the two friends had encountered in the flesh when they were children living for a time under the lock-and-key care of The Brain & Mind Institute which was attached to a hospital.

TC looked confused. "What visitors?"

"Later," said Lennie, to whom the thickening raindrops were appearing as the blood-filled tears of wounded souls sobbing in the heavens. He leaned across and tapped the control arm of the windscreen wiper, sending the blades into a frenzy trying to clear the scene.

But the blades couldn't stop the salty droplets that ran down Lennie's cheeks, spilling into his mouth and onto his tongue with a metallic tang. Amid the twisting shadows and flickering street lights, he turned away from Joe and TC. He wondered what he would do if one day these ectoplasmic visitors become 24-hour-day residents inside his head, along with the Sambuca-inspired electric dogs. Would it be so bad if they never left? Could he put them on a leash? Would they howl day and night? He felt something invisible stroke his hands.

"You'll be right, mate," said Joe. He usually left the touching of Jacks to Lennie, but he lifted a hand from the steering wheel and conspicuously tapped the charm hanging on a bootlace from the rearview mirror. "Let's call Mrs G."

Lennie hit speed-dial and tapped open speaker.

"He's out of intensive care," she said matter-of-factly.

The Firefly itself seemed to sigh.

"Are you boys alright?"

"Yes. Thank you," said Lennie, pleased that the raindrops, at least the ones he could see, were turning from the colour red into pure water.

"The patient is nibbling pulped pumpkin seeds as we speak."

Lennie wiped his eyes. "You're a miracle worker, Mrs G."

"Too right," added Joe.

"We shouldn't leap ahead of ourselves, boys."

"Oh?" said Lennie. "What do you mean?"

Mrs G explained that Rawcus had not yet uttered a meaning-ful word. It appeared he'd lost the ability to speak English and had retreated into the world of regular animals.

Lennie said, "We'll be home shortly, Mrs G."

"Best if you leave him with me tonight. He doesn't need ex-citement right now. My vet friend in the US has given me advice on treatment and helped me mix a herbal sedative. After Rawcus has eaten, we'll get him to sleep."

*

Lennie patted TC's shoulder. "You better stay with us tonight. I feel a lot of weirdness in the air, unnatural things moving. And in the morning, we have that job to crack on with for Pauline at the refuge."

"I don't think I can do the schoolgirl thing. I told you."

"We're all committed now. There's no reverse gear."

"Why do I have to stay at your house?"

The truth was that Lennie didn't want one of the key players in their next *F for Ethics* project getting cold feet and doing a runner. For as small as TC's legs were, he could power them like an Energiser bunny and head in any direction if you didn't grip him by the collar.

Lennie reached into his skull and plucked out the sight of TC laying semi-naked and ball-gagged in the back tray of a small truck on a rainy night much like this one.

Lennie said, "Do you want big Chrissy Enoka snatching you off the street and dragging you around like his man-bag again?"

TC's eyes narrowed. "There's a police manhunt for him and John. Why would he bother with me?"

"Word on the street is that they've traced Pago's last movements back to your work. And they're skinny as rope after crash dieting on the run and disguised themselves. Isn't that right Joe?"

Surprise flickered on Joe's face. He blanked it and lied. "Shit, yeah. Talk is they've split up to throw the plods off their scent. But they want blood over Pago. I've taken to sleeping with a hammer."

TC's body shuddered like he was standing naked in a polar wind.

"Your offer of accommodation sounds terrific," he whispered as if talking more loudly might alert Chris Enoka to his whereabouts.

Joe tapped the power button on the CD player.

Mamma Mia burst from the speakers. Lennie and Joe bobbed and joined the chorus alongside Frida and Agnetha. TC hung from the monkey bar and sipped beer, shaking his head as if his companions needed psychiatric care.

11 - MR CHATTY

IN THE PINK LIGHT of sunrise through a skylight window, Lennie and Joe stepped foggy-eyed downstairs and entered their kitchen. TC, dressed in white underpants and a white polo shirt, was ironing his cream chinos on a fold-out board. Upon the kitchen table stood a tall, glass plunger-pot full of black coffee. Behind the dark tube, a bright yellow feather bobbed in and out of their line of sight.

"Hello!" said Joe, who moved to the side of the pot. "Are you feeling better?"

Rawcus, a blue bandage around both his white wings and torso, was standing on the table chewing kernels of corn off a plate that was elevated by a couple of cookbooks. Rawcus gave Joe a disinterested glance and turned back to his breakfast.

"Good to see you, too," said Joe, whose brow furrowed.

Lennie said to TC, "When did Mr Chatty get back?"

"There was a knock at the door about half-an-hour ago. Gina said she was your neighbour and handed Rawcus to me." TC hissed steam into a trouser leg. "She had to go out."

Lennie nodded at red scratches on TC's chalky-white fore-arms. "What happened there?"

"I don't think he was happy to see me." TC ran the iron over a belt loop. "Gina said his behaviour may be erratic for a few days due to the trauma."

TC pulled on his chinos, careful not to buckle the fresh centre crease in the legs. "She gave me the corn, and a bottle of medicine that he needs to take by dropper every four hours. She'll be back to check the dressing on his wound this afternoon. But you can phone her any time to talk about the patient's prognosis."

Lennie looked at Rawcus eating, and at Joe standing rooted to the spot. He saw a Mexican stand-off. Who would break first? The bird looked up from his corn.

"Giss a kiss, love," said Joe, winking at the bird.

Rawcus turned away, almost tipping over without his wings to balance him, and pecked at a kernel. "Whaat time do you call this!" he screeched.

"Alright," said Joe, holding his hands up in surrender. Rawcus often parroted this line when Joe and Lennie were late home after a day on the tools, or a night at the pub when Rawcus had been left home alone. "We had a job to take care of, and Mrs G had your back."

"Busy boys, hey!" said the bird. "Busy boys, hey!"

TC, sitting on a chair and pulling on his socks, said, "How the hell does he do that?"

"How the *hell*. *D*oes he do that?" cried Rawcus, not looking up from his corn.

Lennie shook his head and rolled his eyes at the bird as if the answer was as mysterious as the meaning of life. "Brain the size of a walnut; the memory of an elephant. I guess when you grow up in a pub, you're born into a world of one-liners. So there's his source material. But it's got me stuffed how he times his delivery."

TC slipped on his tasselled, camel-brown boating shoes. "I read in a science journal that cockatoos have as many neurons in their brains as monkeys and dolphins. Highest intelligence in the animal kingdom."

"Saw that too, mate," said Lennie.

Rawcus twitched his crest, eyes locked on his plate. "Saw that too, mate!"

Joe shook his head impatiently at the high-mindedness of the conversation. "Giss a kiss, love," he said to Rawcus.

Rawcus looked up and eyed the man sideways.

Joe opened his arms.

Rawcus shuffled across the table towards Joe, who kissed the tips of a couple of fingers and patted them on Rawcus's head.

"He's got terrible breath in the mornings," Joe told TC.

"Say that again, and I'll drop ya!" screeched Rawcus, ducking and weaving. "You bagga shit."

Rawcus teetered and began falling, landing on his side on the table before Joe could catch him. Joe propped him back on his claws.

"I'm seein' stars!" cried Rawcus. "You bagga shit!"

TC went wide-eyed.

"The Rose 'n Thistle was a rough pub," Joe explained.

TC curled his little nose. "It's all Aperol Spritz and vegan burgers at the Rose these days. Poet's night on Mondays. Why don't you take him in for reeducation?"

"He's banned," said Joe.

"Why?"

"Abusive language."

Rawcus cocked an eye at TC. "Faark you!"

Lennie tapped his phone and stepped under the kitchen arch into the sitting room. "Yeah, Mrs G. It's Lennie. Thanks for saving Rawcus."

"I had an appointment, love. How is he?"

"Talking again."

"Excellent."

"He's talking a lot."

"A lot?"

"He won't shut up."

"Oh. I'm afraid that's probably the Modafinil wearing off."

"The what?"

"It's mainly prescribed for people who can't stay awake. But they also call it the *genius pill*. It boosts alertness and concentration."

"So you treated him with it?"

"No, of course not, love. But it was my fault."

"How so?"

"He can be a little devil, cant' he? I put him to sleep in a clothes basket at the end of my bed last night. I woke up this morning and he'd tipped himself out and was rifling through a bag on my floor. I have a client I'm trying to help wean off Modafinil and I'd taken her last blister packs to put in a pharmacy bin for safe disposal."

"So he chomped it?"

"He just broke a capsule. It tastes bitter so he only had a micro-dose. Apart from ranting, is he showing any other symptoms?"

"Na. So how does this genius pill work?"

"It heightens brain function. Boosts attention span, memory, learning."

"I could use that."

"Try exercise, love. Call me back if things go off the rails."

Lennie returned to the kitchen.

Rawcus looked at him. "Gidday, bonehead!"

Lennie stroked his hairless head and decided to give the genius pill time to fade. Trying to explain it to the gang would just complicate the morning and detract from the mission ahead.

"TC," said Lennie, scanning the clean and tidy kitchen that bore no sign of yesterday's mayhem with the Tremlett gang. The floor appeared freshly mopped and sparkled. "Your obsessive-compulsive-disorder is worth bottling. Good job."

"Funny thing, isn't it?" TC replied, winding up the cord on the iron. "I only get OCD in kitchens and bathrooms."

Lennie chuckled. He had OCD too, but it mainly applied to the incessant touching of the wooden models of little fingers that he called Lucky Jacks, and a fixation on odd numbers. He reached into his jeans pocket to feel a piece of Bloodwood tree that resembled his dead Aunty Doreen's sixth finger. Doctors had labelled her a *polydactyl* in recognition of her extra digit. These days, Lennie kept a range of Jacks in a box on his bedroom dressing table like another man might keep a collection of watches. The at least daily touch of a Jack provided low-cost insurance against life's risks, and Lennie, as the possibility man in his partnership with Joe – who was better at probability – had made it his duty to always carry a Jack in his pocket, and his Jack-tapping covered both of them.

Lennie heard the sound of bleating sheep. He answered his phone. "Yes, Pauls."

"We are aiming for this weekend," said Pauline Gerrity. "Can you guys make it?"

Lennie eyed TC who was tucking the ironing board back into a gap between the workbench and fridge. "I'm looking at the final piece of the puzzle. Can I call you back in five?"

12 - PAZZO

"YOU REMEMBER Toby Runyon, don't you?" said Lennie, pointing in a teacherly way at a newspaper clipping that was held by a magnet to the door of the fridge.

"Yes," TC grumbled.

"Do I need to read you that story again?"

"Not again!" cried Rawcus. "You fool!"

*

The headline said: *Mystery: Judge's Son Hung By Who?* The text described a prominent Sydney film and TV producer who'd been snatched off a street, encased head-to-toe in black gaffer tape, and suspended as sculpture from a tree branch at night in a busy city restaurant strip.

Two black-clothed artists, the news story said, had hung the installation which they titled, *Cocoon of Man,* and then persuaded bystanders to thrash the cocoon with canes after telling the crowd that it was a mechanical contraption and high-concept work of State-sanctioned street theatre.

Runyon, whose dad was a Federal Court judge, was later cut free from the cocoon and, after a stint in psychiatric care, had confessed to being an amateur boxer on his wife and a keyhole watcher on his pre-teen daughter in the shower. Subsequently, accusations surfaced about other acts of power and privilege that Runyon had visited upon wider society, including upon young women and men who worked underneath him and were now assisting the police to file criminal charges for workplace sexual assaults and bullying.

Lennie and Joe had never been revealed as having a hand in the sculptural events that led to a mental breakdown by Runyon and a confession of his crimes. They had worn gloves and masks. Runyon had now rescinded his confession on his lawyers' legal advice who suggested he plead mental illness at the time every one of the alleged assaults occurred.

*

TC fidgeted and looked down at his shoes. "But playing a school-girl. Must I?"

"Look," said Lennie, visualising TC in a short-sleeved white shirt, dark blue skirt, and long white socks. "Our new target is as greasy as fish and chips. But unlike Runyon, he's on the loose and cockier than a rat with gold teeth."

Lennie reminded TC about what they had learned from Pauline and one of her residents at the refuge: Toby Runyon had secretly provided "technical advice" on digital video production to a psychologist named Dr Ross Fellows who worked for The Child Exploitation Internet Unit of the NSW Police. In addition, Fellows had developed a habit of popping into Pauline's refuge with a big smile, flashing his police ID and trumpeting his academic credentials wanting to interview women and children to further his *field research*.

"You can pull it off," Lennie assured TC.

Rawcus leaned to peck a kernel from his raised plate. "*You can pull it off!*"

TC groaned.

Lennie put his phone on the table, hit speed dial, and tapped open speaker.

"Pauls," said Lennie. "We have our patsy."

"We need a Donna," said Pauline.

TC rubbed his eyes like a child waking. "Patsy may be more apropos. Do you know that the term derives from the Italian word, *pazzo*, meaning madman? Other scholars say patsy is from *paccio*, meaning fool."

Joe shook his head. "Don't overthink it, mate."

"Cut the show pony shit," Lennie added.

"Pull ya head in!" screeched Rawcus.

"TC," said Pauline, "Fellows has a mother-daughter thing. We have the mother, and we thought we had her daughter too. But the mum is terrified about putting her child at risk. And I can't blame her, given what we're learning."

"Put his lights out!" yelled Rawcus.

Joe shook his head at the bird's parroting of a front bar favourite before a punch-up. He drilled Rawcus with a death stare. "Put a sock in it, please mate."

Pauline resumed. "TC, this man is endlessly active and he's become untouchable by the law because of his job as an insider."

TC said, "You've given him the codename, Mr Teflon. Yes?"

"That was the boys' idea. They tell me you can do this job for us with your eyes closed. But don't close your eyes...and guys, Carol is trying to arrange dinner with Fellows tonight. I'll come back to you when I know where. But her objective is to set up a family stay with him at his beach house. This weekend if she can. I'll keep you posted."

Pauline hung up.

Joe sighed. *Carol* was a codename too, but she was a real mother, and so was her daughter. Like her mum, the twelve-year-old was a feisty kid who could punch above her weight; Joe had been sure of that after meeting her. And he would have covered her like a nuke-proof force field on this operation. But Joe looked at Rawcus, and his bandaged torso, and he realised that his mighty defences had failed the bird, almost fatally. Would he fail TC too?

Lennie poured a cup of coffee from the plunger pot and looked at TC. "Have you ever worn a schoolgirl's uniform? And don't lie – because when you do your eyelids twitch."

"My sister's," said TC, his eyelids as still as stone.

"How often?"

"Come on, Lennie."

"You know the drill then."

"I didn't step outside her bedroom."

"Now's your chance."

TC squinted. "Will this *schoolgirl* be in danger?"

13 - TRAPDOOR

"WHEN YOU'RE dealing with a snake," said Lennie, "stay away from its head."

TC shuddered.

"Remember how you handled Pago?" Lennie added reassuringly, recalling that the pint-sized scientist had a pretty good record of dealing with lethal threats.

Months ago, TC had been kidnapped by the murderous third brother in line to the Enoka Family throne. He'd turned the tables on the giant Pacific Islander by cooking up a story about hidden treasure, a tale that sent Pago Enoka running into a swinging steel gate, booby-trapped with spikes that had fatally impaled him at a bush property called, *The End of the World*.

Lennie thought about how Pago's demise had fused him, Joe, and TC into the prongs of a trident of sorts, given that he and Joe had constructed the gate which was designed to fortress a secret botanical project they had embarked upon with TC as an expert consultant.

It was codenamed *Fountain of Youth,* or FOY for short, and the idea was to grow plants to create a chemical compound that could slow, and even reverse, the ageing process, and potentially destroy cancerous tumours "in both mice and men", as TC had put it. Pago's departure to the netherworld, and a raid by some burglars, had put FOY on hold.

Now, in the kitchen, TC sighed. "Yeah, well I was living a charmed life – until Chris and John showed up." TC massaged his jaw where the two surviving Enoka brothers had ball-gagged him after Pago disappeared.

"You're with me and Joe now," said Lennie. "You've heard of safety in numbers?"

"So we're like brothers?" said TC.

Lennie looked TC up and down. "I always wanted a sister."

Joe looked rueful. "I had one of those."

"Had?" said TC.

"She went missing twenty years ago," said Joe, thinking that his big sister might still be around if she'd found shelter in the sort of place that Pauline operated. "Just turned fifteen."

"OK, baby bro," said Lennie, nodding at TC. "Let's get to work."

"How?"

"Into the hole," said Joe. "At least you won't have any trouble getting inside."

TC tried to bolt, but Joe caught him by the polo shirt collar, which stretched quite a bit.

Rawcus prowled the kitchen table, eyeing his claws as he stepped. "Watch 'em! Don't go there, mate!"

"Trust," said Joe. "And you," he said, turning to Rawcus, "I dunno what's happened since you got shot, but if you keep that stuff up, you're going back to Mrs G's."

Rawcus gave Joe a filthy look but kept his beak shut.

Lennie stroked his jaw, pondering a new mystery: could the knock upon Rawcus's head, and the chemistry of the genius pill, lead to a permanent brain change, the cracking open of a cerebral pathway to another consciousness? Where might this lead? Original thought and expansive expression? My God, Lennie wondered, will Rawcus be sneaking into adult literacy class on Joe's shoulder next, pretending he's just there for the ride before he springs the truth on the class? He might even get ambitions to be a teacher; the bird certainly had the ego for it.

Joe looked up at the clock on the wall, its second hand juddering around the dial. "It's all in the timing."

Lennie and Joe winked at each other. Joe swooped, scooping Rawcus gently off the table, keeping his fingers out of beak range. Lennie opened an empty kitchen cupboard that had a see-through, wire-mesh door.

"Help! Help!" the bird cried. "Murder!"

Joe put Rawcus in the cupboard and hastily closed the door. "You need to chill out," Joe said into the mesh. "We'll be back soon." He turned a key that was in the door lock.

TC shook his head. "You need a tranquiliser gun."

To obscenity-ridden, high-pitched accusations of homicide, Lennie led TC sandwiched by Joe through the kitchen into the back garden.

Joe closed the door. Bruce, the skinny black cat, was sunbaking atop a fat joist of the picket fence; he put his good eye suspiciously on Joe.

Joe said to the cat, "Your mate's just having a bad day. He'll come good after a rest."

The cat winked.

"We're letting you in on a family secret," Lennie said to their nervous guest as they stepped along the path between house and garden.

Inside the garden shed, TC looked aghast at the old dentist's chair. "You don't do each other's teeth, do you?"

Lennie smiled, exposing a gap where an incisor had been. He opened a cupboard door and pointed at a bottle of household bleach, a bottle of isopropyl alcohol, a stainless steel cocktail shaker, and a full-face respirator mask. "After a snort of home-made chloroform, you won't feel a thing, bro."

"I've just had a check-up and clean, thanks." TC pressed his lips tight.

Lennie closed the cupboard. "Next time then."

Joe bent his knees, kept his back straight, and grasped the foot of the electric chair; Lennie grabbed the headrest. They lifted it off a grease-stained rug.

TC relaxed. "Where'd you get that thing? I mean, what's it for?"

The chair-lifters put it down beside the rug.

Lennie said, "A few months ago, Firefly Electrics won a contract to install a new batch of chairs for the *Smile for Life* chain of dentist surgeries. We got to keep this old one."

Joe said, "Thought we'd give it a clean and put it in the lounge room. You know, for watching TV, or having a snooze. But it turned out to be a pretty good quizmaster for that prick Tremlett, hey?"

Joe bent down and rolled up the floor rug, revealing a rusty trapdoor.

TC went wide-eyed. "That the hole?"

Lennie grabbed a crowbar that was hanging from a nail on the wall. He shoved the bar's beak into a gap between the floor and trapdoor rim and levered the steel hatch up enough for Joe to slip some fingers in and haul it open.

"My grandad built this," said Lennie. "It was rusted tight as a priest's wallet for decades."

"Where does it go?" said TC.

"Joe and I have cleaned out an old room near the top level. Grandad's map says further down there's a tunnel to an old coal mine."

"Seriously?"

"These parts of the city were full of coal mines once. Grandad reckoned this one fed boilers in steam-driven local factories last century. On paper, it pops into a canal near the railway station up the street."

"Cool," said TC. "So an escape hatch for local crims, yes?"

"Be polite," said Lennie, peering into the black hole.

TC enthused, "Could be a tourism business in it. Got to be ghost stories floating around."

"We got about fifty metres down but hit a cave-in."

"Jesus," said TC, reeling back from the open trapdoor. "The earth could swallow us at any moment!"

"So could the universe," said Lennie. "Get in."

"No."

"Oh, for God's sake," said Lennie, who stepped onto the metal rungs of a ladder built into the wall of the tunnel. A light flicked on below his feet.

Joe hipped TC towards the hole. "It's safe as houses, mate. Go for it."

"I'll get dirty," said TC, eyeing his neatly pressed chinos. He stroked his white polo shirt.

"Hells Bells," said Joe, opening a cupboard and extracting a full-body, paper hazard-suit. "Here!"

TC donned the overalls. He took a while to roll back the sleeves and trouser legs. He backed down the ladder, followed by Joe.

The small room cut into the side of the tunnel was illuminated with a string of white globes hooked to the rough-hewn sandstone walls. Joe had to stoop to get in.

The three stood in front of a workbench fitted against a wall. They gazed at five wigs of human-looking hair that were perched on clear glass skulls atop the bench. Short blond; wavy long black; shoulder-length chestnut; Caesar-cut grey; and a blue-green moptop.

"Party hat," said Lennie, patting the moptop.

TC scanned the room, bringing his eyes to rest on a suitcase-sized metal box sitting on the floor in a corner. On its door, there were several concentric ring-dials with numbers.

"Is that where you keep the gold the Enokas are after? 'cause you didn't give away all the stuff you got off that dodgy accountant's boat, did you?"

Joe combed his red hair with his fingers but they got stuck in the knots. "This isn't a quiz show, mate."

"I think TC would look best in this one," said Lennie, putting onto his own shaved skull the chestnut wig that was parted in the middle and fell below his jawline.

TC cringed: "Are these handmade...homemade? They look very realistic."

"Do you think we scalp people?" said Lennie.

TC looked unsure.

"You might as well know the truth," said Lennie. "We keep the heads in here." He spun the dials on the door of the metal safe and swung it open.

TC grabbed his chest as if trying to stop his heart from leaping through his ribcage.

Lennie reached into the novelty fridge and pulled out a can of Cutters Lager. "Anyone for a coldie?"

Joe took a beer and smiled at the sight of Lennie with hair on his head. His friend could grow it, but he chose to shave it because a local priest named Father Francesco had liked to run his fingers through Lennie's schoolboy locks.

"Mate," Joe said thoughtfully, snapping the cap on the can and taking a closer look at Lennie. "You look like that sooky country and western singer. What's his name? Married to Hollywood Nicole."

"You mean that little rooster Keith Bourbon?"

Lennie checked his reflection in a wall mirror, stroking the straight strands away from his cheeks. "Ah, fuck the Grand Ole Opry." He plopped the wig on TC's head.

TC whipped the hair-hat off as if it was crawling with fleas. He examined its scalp. After a few moments, apparently satisfied that its skin was not organic, he put it back on his head and leaned forward so the hair veiled most of his face.

"Hello, Donna," said Lennie. "How was school today?"

TC studied himself in the mirror and sighed. "It might work." He pouted. "Guess I'll have a beer too, please."

Lennie opened the fridge.

TC spied on a shelf below the Cutters Lager a handful of black-covered notebooks stacked inside a transparent plastic bag. "Why keep books in a fridge?"

"What do you reckon, Joe," said Lennie. "Shall we tell him?"

Joe looked thoughtful and took a coin from his pocket. He flipped it into the black space of the tunnel beside the room. It clanged on the metal rungs and plunged into silence. "If you blab, TC, you'll follow the money as sure as night follows day."

"I don't need to know anymore," said TC, pulling off the wig. He put the unopened beer on the bench. "I talk too much when I drink."

Lennie grinned. "Too late, bro." He lifted the bag of notebooks from the fridge and swung it to and fro. "Our life story is in here. The *up to now* bit, anyway."

TC looked puzzled.

Joe shook his head. "Lennie thinks he's a writer."

"Well, I'm giving it a crack," said Lennie. "Anyway, now that you're in the fold, TC, you have a duty."

"I hate responsibilities. You know that's why I live alone."

Joe grinned. "Oh, it's a choice thing."

Lennie said, "I've written about our adventures, but they have to stay top secret, probably until we die. Because if the cops get hold of them, we'll probably get life sentences, or as good as. And we're allergic to cages."

TC shook his head. "So why take the risk?"

"Because some stories need telling."

"Shit, Lennie. Am I in there?"

"Only in book two."

"Oh, for God's sake. The stuff about Pago Enoka?" TC grabbed the beer and snapped the cap.

"It's riveting stuff. What's called a page-turner in the trade."

"Great." TC guzzled lager.

Lennie put the bag back in the fridge.

TC patted foam off his lips. "Is that gold in the veggie crisper?"

Lennie closed the door.

TC sipped then sighed. "So what's my duty, as you call it?"

"If we cark it before you do, you have to come down here and save the family silver, so to speak."

"What's the point if we are the only ones who ever read the stories?"

"Ah, no wonder you got into uni, TC. Fact is, I'm in the process of switching all the names in the books to pseudonyms to protect the players. Then I'll look for a publisher, or I might even do it myself." Lennie sipped. "You know, the more I think about it, fuck the gatekeepers. I could blast this stuff across the internet with a few keyboard clicks."

Joe lifted his beer. "Fuck the gatekeepers."

Lennie grinned. "But right now, this shit could blow up in our faces because it's fact dressed up as fiction, and the dress is a bit thin."

TC rolled his eyes. "Does your friend Pauline know about this? Is she in it?"

"She's my editor," said Lennie. "Joe's a plot consultant."

"You're insane," said TC. "I suppose you have a muse too?"

"Rawcus."

"Oh, my giddy aunt." TC gulped lager.

Lennie drained his beer and crushed the can between his palms. He tucked the wodge of metal in his back pocket. "Recycling," he said. "Time to go."

They tidied the room, bagged TC's wig, and climbed up the stairs.

In the house, they phoned Pauline for advice. She gave them the address of a school uniform shop. She also briefed them on the conversation she'd just had with Carol. She was dining with Fellows this evening. And she was scared.

14 - NOT ALL FATHERS ARE THE SAME

BEHIND THE TINTED WINDOWS of his shiny BMW four-wheel-drive, child psychologist, Dr Ross Fellows, PhD, changed lanes and practiced his happy-go-lucky *Will Carter* face in the rear-vision mirror. But he couldn't change the fact that he hated Japanese food and worried that he might inadvertently turn his nose up at the restaurant to which he was heading.

On the upside, he thought, the *Fuji* sounded like an old fashioned brand of film stock from the days before digital cameras. He had loved voyaging into the otherworld of infra-red light in a darkened room and drawing into his nostrils the intoxicating fumes of ammonia and sulphur that wafted from a photopaper bath.

As a fourteen-year-old, his parents had given him a manually operated 35mm, single-lens-reflex camera. It was sensuous using his hands to focus the lens, to set the aperture, to click a button and hear the clunk of the shutter, to thumb-crank a lever that rolled the film to set up the next shot. But digital tech had its advantages too. It was incredibly easy for a lone man to make brilliantly detailed motion pictures...

Seated inside the *Fuji*, he faced Carol across a black lacquered wooden table. A candlelit paper lantern immersed them in ruby-coloured light. The illumination reminded him of a photographic darkroom and comforted him.

"So," he said. "You like the beach, Carol?"

"My daughter does," Carol replied. "My skin's prone to burn, but I do love the sensation of the surf on my skin."

Fellows used chopsticks to dunk a piece of raw, pink tuna into a shallow dish of soy sauce. He soaked the flesh in the salty black liquid to mask the hideous taste.

"I grew up on the beach," he said. "At a place called Cottesloe in Perth. Do you know it?"

"No. I've never been to Western Australia."

"Oh, it's very beautiful, watching the sun set over the Indian Ocean. I guess most Australians live on the east of the continent, so they've never had that pleasure."

"I'd like to go there one day."

Fellows studied Carol for telltale signs: scratching her nose; tugging an ear lobe, avoiding eye contact. She'd done none of those things. He grew confident that she was telling the truth. But Carol wore false eyelashes. Mm. He pondered. No, that wasn't necessarily an indicator of dishonesty. It was more an indicator of medium-level vanity. And vanity he could exploit.

He said, "We moved to Sydney about two years ago."

"We?"

"It didn't work out. My wife, ex-wife I mean, is married again. She has primary custody of Helen. I'm a Mr Weekend Dad, and after school sometimes."

"You'd like to see more of her then?"

"Of course. You just love them, don't you? There's no debate. It's not optional."

"Not all fathers are the same."

"Thank god for that," he said, working hard to shape his mouth into a smile.

Carol nodded. "You know I'm a nurse. What do you do for work, Will?"

"Nothing exciting, I'm afraid. I work in an office. An insurance claims assessor."

"Oh. So if I dent my car on a lampost, and I say someone else did it, you'll put me under the hot lights to see if I'm fibbing."

"Close. I specialise in arson. House fires, industrial fires. That sort of thing."

"So you'd have contacts with the police?"

"Yes, I do. Just a few. What about you?"

"You mean, do I know any policemen? No, I stay as far away from the law as possible."

"Excellent idea," he said. "Now. When are we going to introduce our kids?"

She smiled: "Whenever it suits you, Will."

He shifted uncomfortably. Was she seeing through him? He looked into her eyes and smiled back. Had she been physically damaged in some way? To hell with it, he thought. He was feeling frisky; he would chance his arm with an early charge from the trenches.

"How about this weekend?" he said. "Our beach house is only a few hours south of Sydney. I have a big car. I can drive us all."

"That's very generous, Will. I'll talk to Donna and come back to you as soon as I can."

After dinner, he insisted on driving Carol home to Summer Hill. He didn't say so, of course, but he wanted to look at where she lived, to run another test on her credibility. The traffic was thin at ten o'clock at night and they had a jolly chat about their favourite film and TV shows, about which he lied quite well, he thought. He loathed – absolutely loathed – Agatha Christie's detective stories; why would anyone ever confess to anything under moderate heat from a half-baked gumshoe? For God's sake, you just deny, deny, deny. Build an alternative reality and take the rest of the world into it with you. Donald Trump, now there was a man to be admired – just not out loud. No, don't express any political opinions at all in public; it just helps others build a profile of you.

Carol asked him to drop her on the side of a road at a bus stop near a mix of shops and residential housing. The residences were mostly single-level, wide-fronted, turn-of-the-Twentieth-Century brick bungalows.

She stepped from his car onto the grass verge and said through the open passenger door: "Thanks for dinner, Will. I'll be in touch about this weekend. Soon."

He watched Carol open a gate in front of a large, shabby house perched on a rise. She climbed up a handful of steps to the wide, covered veranda. At the top of the steps, she turned and waved. He waved – and waited.

15 - FARADAY'S CAGE

BACKING INTO the cool shadows of the veranda, Carol took a handkerchief from her bag and dabbed beads of sweat on her upper lip and forehead. She plucked out her phone and used fingerprint ID to open it. Her trembling thumb hovered over a number. She stepped forward and pressed the door buzzer of the house she did not know.

A porch light blinked on. The front door lock clicked. She glanced back towards Fellows.

She gasped. The red tail lights of his car were vanishing up the street. A bus was making a passenger drop where Fellows had lurked. The hinges on the front door of the house creaked.

"Yes?" growled a squint-eyed, grey-haired, hollow-cheeked man. He was wearing a brown towelling dressing gown and beige slippers. A small, scruffy dog yapped behind his ankles.

"I'm sorry," said Carol. "I must have the wrong address."

The man sniffed as if there was a bad smell and closed his door. The dog kept yapping. Carol moved quickly back down the steps, through the gate, and onto the footpath, hot-footing away. Sheltering behind a tree trunk, she glanced back at the road.

"Oh, no," she hissed. Fellows' car was rolling to a stop on the opposite side of the street. His driver's side window came down. He looked at the house Carol had walked up to.

Ahead of her, a dozen or so steps away, there was a narrow, dark public footpath between two homes. Trying to stay in the shadow of the tree to block Fellows' line of sight, Carol scampered towards the path and ducked in. She paused, peeping back at Fellows.

*

Fellows looked across the road at the house inside which Carol said she rented rooms for herself and Donna. It looked big enough to be a boarding house, he thought. The lights of a TV flickered behind a lace-curtained window. Should he park and knock on the door? No, that would appear too keen, desperate even, and might frighten her off. Maybe he could just sneak up and have a peek through the window. Yes.

But what if he was caught? No.

He drove on. He stopped at a set of traffic lights and fingered a text message into his phone: "*Sleep tight, Carol. X. Will.*"

*

On the dimly-lit footpath between the houses, Carol's phone pinged. She read his message and replied: "*You too. X, Carol*".

She walked away from the main street and hit speed dial. While speaking, she came to a sleepy street lined with parked cars, a couple of boats on trailers, and a few small trucks. She hung up and leaned in shadow against the trunk of a tree.

A dog barked. A baby cried. A man yelled. A fruit bat launched from a branch above her and winged into the moonlit sky...the headlamps of an approaching car caught her. Carol's heart hammered.

A white tradesman's van parked beside her. The side door slid open. A folded wheelchair was strapped against a wall. She climbed into the van.

"Please," said Lennie, pointing for Carol to sit in an empty armchair in the rear end of the Firefly. She sat. He hurled the slider shut.

"You're safe now, darling," said Pauline, using her hands to swivel her lifeless legs to the side of the front passenger seat so she could have eye contact with Carol.

"I'm shaking," said Carol, holding up her hands.

"Here," said Lennie, unscrewing the top of a thermos flask. "Hot chocolate made with eighty-five percent cocoa and full-cream milk. My Aunty Doreen's trademark recipe."

He poured into the thermos-top cup and handed it to Carol. Headlights streamed through the Firefly's windscreen.

Carol slopped her drink. "Is that him? Maybe he has his police force friends tracking my phone."

The car went by.

Lennie stroked his chin. "I don't think Mr Teflon is the type to involve a team in his capers. More a lone wolf. But let's err on the side of caution, hey?"

He opened a drawer on a wall cabinet and extracted a copper box the size of a paperback novel. "Pop your phone in here, Carol."

"What is it?"

"A Firefly Electrics Faraday Cage. No signals get in, no signals get out. They're for sale on our website."

Carol placed her phone into the box. Lennie shut the lid.

Joe looked in the rear vision mirror. "You can save yourself a hundred bucks and wrap your blower in kitchen foil. Does the same trick for a fraction of the price."

"Thanks," Lennie grumbled. "You really know how to kill a business idea."

Pauline said, "Who'd want a box like that? Be a small market wouldn't it? Criminals, terrorists?"

"Hello!" said Lennie, indignantly. "I kid you not, I was talking to a friend the other day and she said out loud "do you know a good psychologist?" and Siri popped up on her phone and recommended a medical centre around the corner. Creepy, or what?"

Carol smiled and sipped her drink. "When do I meet my new daughter?"

16 - CHILDHOOD

FELLOWS CHECKED the time on his phone as he entered his flat: 11.18pm. Too early. He was a post-midnight sleeper and a tad superstitious about hitting the sack prior to the clock's turn between night and day.

He pulled open the balcony doors and welcomed a soft breeze. Across the road, surf walloped in white lines atop dark water, sounding like artillery fire. He knew this thump and rumble from his training in the Army Reserve. What a terrific idea that had been. The stint of national service looked fantastic on his CV when he applied for his job as an in-house psychologist with the police force, joining a task force inside the Child Exploitation Internet Unit. Dr Ross Fellows: patriot! Defender of the people!

God, he thought, the people he had come across since landing his law enforcement job. It was enough to do your head in. The money they would pay for live streaming video was obscene. The content they shared made the hairs on his neck stand up.

And the idiocy of some human beings. A syndicate of morons had just been arrested for trying to import a thousand inflatable sex dolls from a factory in Shanghai, owned by the family of a Chinese Communist Party chief. The importers claimed the child-sized imitations of boys and girls were a factory error, and that the associated invoices, detailing their mini-measurements, were a computer glitch. That business was sunk now, Fellows told himself. Best not to think about it.

Fellows grabbed a beer from the kitchen fridge and plonked back on the sofa in his sitting room.

He sipped. Ha. How the world is changing. Hard to keep up. These days, old-fashioned hard storage was coming back into vogue – especially now that the global internet police were getting better at breaking into the *dark web* of online paedophile networks. Plenty of viewers and content creators were going to jail for long stretches. You didn't need to be an Einstein or an Epstein or in Fellows' job to know this. The international busts were routinely reported in the media.

But it didn't stop the perps, did it? Nothing stops the perpetrators! A digital trail online was very hard to cover up, and becoming harder with the erosion of data protection laws that the age of terrorism had given birth to. Not to mention sneaky police posing online as children. Yes, he had to concede, going online had become very risky business. Very. Oh, fuck it...he'd just have a quick look at the new movie from Berlin. On the big TV screen.

Better close the balcony doors and pull the blackout curtains, and wear his headset to listen to the audio in crystal clear privacy. Don't want to alert the nosy fucking neighbours. That new couple next door and their licky dog were pains in the arse. The poodle was cute though.

He went to the kitchen and pulled a wooden breadboard from a shelf. Its chessboard-patterned surface was scarred with knife marks. It's amazing, he thought, what a skilled craftsman can do if you give them a decent brief.

"A masterstroke," he muttered, recalling his idea of roughing up the cutting surface with real knife marks and staining it by actually using it to prepare food. The woodworker he'd commissioned had created internal chambers that were virtually impossible to detect. And it was just as amazing how many thousands of hours of video he could store on the two, single terabyte flash drives he kept in waterproof wraps in the chambers.

He pulled a paperclip from his wallet, bent it open, and popped a nib into a tiny hole on one edge of the breadboard. He pressed, triggering a lock as small and neat as any phone's SIM card slot. A tray popped out. Snug inside it lay the matchbox-sized flash drives, one white and one black. He selected white. He plugged it into the USB port on the side of his TV screen.

Fellows lay on his sofa clutching his beer and a bowl of salt and vinegar potato chips. He put his spectacles on and picked up the remote control. The movie, titled *Crofts 2.0,* starred a cream-skinned girl with curly blond hair cuddling a Samoyed dog with a brilliant white coat. The girl and the dog, he guessed, were about the same age. Five or six. The handler was a man of about Fellows' age.

Through his experience with the child porn crime unit, and the educational opportunities that arose for him through its sister organisations in the US and UK in particular, he had built unique knowledge and skills. He knew how the makers of movies like *Crofts 2.0* got their wares through Border Force and

Customs to their customers – or failed, and oh, wasn't failure fundamental to learning. He'd learned how they billed them too, and how they retained confidentiality for all involved. The market for fresh, imaginative content of this type was insatiable. The suppliers, he had learned, saw themselves as entrepreneurs simply catering to market demand. In essence, it was a chicken and egg thing. The simple fact was: it exists. And it always would, as long as humans lived.

Fellows' phone beeped. A text from Carol: *Donna and I are good for this weekend. A friend has agreed to lend me a car. Please send me the address, and what time to arrive on Friday, and we'll meet you and Helen there. I hope you don't mind about the car, but we like our independence. X, Carol.*

17 - MILO WAGNER

LENNIE, JOE, AND TC packed mini-cameras, batteries, TC's wig, and other mission-critical gear into the Firefly on the street in front of their terrace house. They went back inside.

"Great friend, you are!" cried Rawcus as Joe stepped into the kitchen. The bird paced the table.

"Sorry, mate. But someone has to stay home to guard the fort." Joe moved to stroke Rawcus's crest.

Still wearing a torso bandage but with his wings set free, Rawcus nipped Joe's finger with fierce intent as if to prove he had recovered enough for whatever mission they were heading out on. But his beak didn't break Joe's skin as it usually did when applied with such effort.

As Rawcus sulked at his failed fitness test, Joe pulled his phone from his pocket and dialled.

"Morning, Mrs G. You far away?"

"Just doing my morning drop-offs, Joe. I'll pop over and collect Rawcus as soon as I get home."

"So there's plenty of people who still need your stuff then?"

"The government might have legalised medicinal cannabis, love. But it can cost a fortune if you're on a budget, which most of my patients are. And pharma companies don't do home delivery."

"You're a saint."

"Halos are for rainbows, Joe. I'm just doing what I can."

"Pain can be a terrible thing, Mrs G. And you help for free."

"Well, a lot more people would be suffering if you boys hadn't helped me build that garden, and to keep it running. So I want you to promise me something."

"Ooh. This sounds serious."

"Whatever you two are doing, you must come home safe and sound because I need you. *We* need you."

"Don't you sweat, Mrs G. We're not doing anything dangerous."

"You're not a good fibber, love."

He hung up. Rawcus sidled up to Joe's spare hand and closed his beak on a little finger. He failed to make a dent. "Nice try," said Joe, who carried a large bag of light bulbs out to the van.

Friday was a workday so TC phoned his boss at a medical research lab to say he was still sick from the gastro bug that had floored him the day before.

In the sitting room, Lennie stuffed DS Tremlett's pistol in a backpack and wrestled with thoughts about the possibility that Tremlett, or his mates, might cruise by while they were out and toss a Molotov cocktail through the front window. At least Rawcus would be next door, and the new sprinkler systems and back-to-base fire alarms they had installed in Mrs G's house too should kick into action.

TC, standing beside Lennie, was packing cheese sandwiches into a zip-top cooler for a picnic en route down the south coast.

Lennie kept his mouth shut about the Molotov idea in order not to put a match to generalised anxiety among the team. Instead, he touched the Jack inside his pocket and felt a bit better. He also felt eyes upon him and turned to face the doorway to the kitchen.

"I'm no bird!" cried Rawcus, who flicked his beak angrily against a vase of dried flowers that toppled on the table.

The skin crawled on Lennie's freshly shaven scalp. He turned to TC, "Did you hear what he just said?"

"*Rack-rack-rack,*" TC replied, zipping the cooler shut.

Lennie realised that TC wasn't a trained cockatoo listener or speaker. The words "I'm no bird" had sounded as clear as a bicycle bell to Lennie. He called out, "There's a book about Australian native birds here on the coffee table. You'll find your family in it."

TC's brow furrowed. "Have you been drinking?"

"I wasn't talking to you."

Lennie opened the bird book to the page of illustrated cockatoos and held it splayed by placing an ashtray on the centrefold. "I think Rawcus is suffering an identity crisis after his brush with death. He needs to re-learn his place in the world."

"Can he actually read?"

"Who knows?" Lennie replied. He didn't have time to explain the genius pill. And besides, TC was the sort of character who'd race next door and hound Mrs G for a sample. "But what's the downside of assuming he can?"

"Mm," said TC, pondering. "I saw that Margaret Fulton cookbook in the kitchen. Maybe he'll bake a cake for us while we're out."

"Fuck you, TC."

"Let's go, you idiots," said Joe, who'd been standing in the doorway listening.

"I mean it," said Lennie. "That fall has changed him."

Joe stepped into the kitchen and moved to pat Rawcus good-bye, but the bird turned his back. "See you soon, matey," said Joe, ruffling the bird's crest.

As they shut the front door, Joe thought he heard "Giss a kiss, love" echo behind it, but he didn't have time for what he'd seen kids and parents do at the school gate.

Joe drove them to the school uniform shop that Pauline recommended. Lennie and TC went inside and spoke to a woman behind the counter. They gave her the name of a girl's school.

"What size is your niece?" she asked.

Lennie nodded at TC. "About the same size as my friend as a matter of fact."

TC scowled as the woman measured him with a tape. They chose a tunic and added a school backpack, black lace-up shoes, and white socks.

When Lennie paid with cash, the woman's face looked like she'd seen it all before.

After shopping, they visited TC's flat so he could pack an overnight bag. TC had the brainwave of adding to the Fellows operation some "lollies" that he'd cooked up by happy chance a few days ago in his home lab. It was an idea which radiated colourful possibilities for the mission ahead and to which Lennie and Joe responded with enthusiasm, not least because they thought they might get a lolly too at the end of the day.

They headed for Pauline's newly purchased apartment in nearby Surry Hills, rode a lift to the first floor, and buzzed the bell. Carol opened the door.

Pauline was sitting in her wheelchair in the open-plan kitchen cum living room, her fair hair pulled into a ponytail, her lips glossy with red lipstick, her blue eyes shining. Her smile was nearly as wide as her face.

"Are you still off the booze?" said Joe, hugging Pauline from the side.

"Does it show?"

Joe gave a thumbs-up.

"You should try it," she said.

"I have."

Lennie leaned down and kissed her cheek. He introduced TC.

"This is very nice, but what about that lift?" said Lennie, surveying the main room of the art-nouveau flat which featured ceilings decorated with plaster grapevines and roses.

"I knew you'd say that. There's a ramp at the end of the corridor outside that goes straight down to the street. If there's a fire, I can be out in a jiffy."

"He does fuss," said Joe, who'd been thinking exactly the same thing.

Lennie made a mental note to check the smoke alarms on their return. He nodded at TC. "What do you think of Little Miss Muffet?"

Carol offered her hands to TC.

TC placed the shopping bags holding his school clothes on the floor and put his hands in Carol's. She inspected his fingernails and declared they could use some nail polish, but nothing too loud. She was a twelve-year-old after all.

Pauline wheel-turned to face TC who stood just a tad higher than her. "It's brave of you to volunteer, Milo Wagner."

TC bit his lip.

"I looked you up online," Pauline said. "You have quite the pedigree. A university medal too. How did you come to be friends with a couple of sparkies?"

"They fixed my lights once."

Joe reached down and ruffled TC's hair. "Milo, how sweet."

TC screwed up his ski-slope nose. "TC is fine."

Lennie stepped across the room and peered through the glass balcony doors at a café across the street. "Carol, is that where you met Fellows, or whatever he's calling himself at the moment?"

"Yes," she said. "He's been using *Will Carter* for weeks now."

"We'd better hit the road soon," said Joe, looking at a kookaburra clock on the wall. "We need to get to that beach house well before he does so we can set things up."

Lennie nodded. "Pauls, can TC use your bedroom to get changed? We should give him and Carol a screen test before we go. Though we did some dry runs at home and *Donna* here scored high."

Minutes later, a shy, skinny girl shuffled in front of the four adults. She was dressed in a crisp, blue-and-white checked tunic worn over a white, short-sleeved shirt with a flattened wing collar. On her feet were shiny, black, lace-up shoes worn over white, calf-length socks. Her hair was straight and shoulder-length, parted down the middle.

Carol and Pauline set to work on TC's finishing touches: faint eyeliner on the lower lids; dabs of flesh-coloured powder on the cheeks and nose to smooth the complexion; clear lip gloss; clear polish on her clipped nails.

They were creating a budding pre-teen not a strawberry tart, Pauline reminded them, and Fellows was attracted to clean, un-ripened fruit.

"It won't work, said TC, flicking his hair petulantly in front of a wall mirror.

"Very good," said Pauline, appearing impressed with TC's expression of adolescent moodiness.

"I mean it!" TC insisted. "He'd have to be half-blind to fall for this."

Carol brightened. "He does wear reading glasses. Thick lenses. He needed them for the restaurant menu."

Lennie scratched his chin. "You know what they say: *break glass in case of emergency.*"

TC grizzled. "So I'm meant to punch him in the face?"

"Voice?" said Joe.

"It's OK," said Pauline. "But if TC says too much, it might fall off a cliff."

TC slumped in an armchair. "I told you this was insane."

Carol said, "Gum. We'll get you some chewing gum, Milo. You can be a surly little so-and-so. Then you can leave most of the talking to me."

"Posture?" said Lennie. "What do you think, mum?"

Carol studied TC. "You can't sit with your legs apart like that. Keep them closed, at first anyway."

Lennie watched Carol mentoring TC. She was wearing a floral-print, sleeveless frock in hues of green, with black leather pumps on her feet. Her mousy-brown hair fell loose to her shoulders. She had a pixie-like face that wasn't too bad a match with TC's, especially in the dull light in the flat. She insisted that TC shave the downy hairs off his forearms.

Lennie said, "Let's hit the road."

*

Carol and TC climbed into an old, white Toyota Corolla that Lennie and Joe had exchanged without paperwork for a few kilos of Mars Grass via a friend who operated a motor mechanic's workshop.

Joe, Lennie, and Pauline headed for the Firefly. Joe helped Pauline into the front passenger seat while Lennie folded her wheelchair and placed it in the back, securing it to a wall with a strap. He sat on his Aunty D's old armchair in the deep rear of the van.

Led by the Firefly, the convoy headed for the Pacific Highway and the south coast.

As they moved through the suburbs, Lennie used alcohol wet-wipes and a scrap of T-shirt to polish any fingerprints off Tremlett's semi-automatic pistol. There were five cartridges in the magazine. He wrapped the gun in the rag and tucked it in his backpack.

"So, Pauls," said Lennie, sliding low in the armchair with his legs stretched and feet resting on a twenty-four-can drink cooler. "Refresh us on our fellow's latest modus operandi."

"Well," said Pauline. "Mr Fellows is a family man, as you know. He likes broken ones. He pretends he's the glue who can fix them."

"The shit you see in that refuge, Pauls, it must make your head spin."

"Some of it would curl your hair, Lennie. If you bothered to grow it."

Lennie massaged his scalp. A sick feeling churned in his solar plexus. He could feel Farther Francesco's fingers inside his schoolboy locks. He said, "Can we go back a step?"

"Where to?"

"With Tracy Jarvis and her case against Fellows. Any intel on what happened to her eyewitness?"

"Nothing," said Pauline. "She just vanished."

"Do you reckon Fellows bumped her off?"

"Who knows, Lennie. Some people just want to disappear and they're good at it."

"It got Fellows off the hook though, didn't it? What did the Public Prosecutor's Office say?"

"There was no way they could proceed with a sexual assault case against a senior police force employee without at least one person to back up Tracy's claims. Tracy on her own, with her junkie history, would have been torn to pieces by the defence."

Joe said, "Where's Tracy now?"

18 - MISS MUNCH

"POLARIS HOUSE, JOE."

Pauline's words caused Joe's throat to feel dry and itchy. He recalled how he'd been plucked out of school with Lennie and locked for a month in the same place. Then it had been called The Mind & Brain Institute, and decades before that the Greentree Lunatic Asylum.

"Her girls?" he asked.

"Foster care."

Entering the motorway, Joe glanced into his outside rearview mirror. The white Corolla was in it. He drifted the Firefly to the cruising lane and Carol tucked in behind him.

The van's tyres hummed on the smooth tar. Pauline and Lennie began to doze.

Joe kept his eyes on the road, but his mind's eye strayed into the world of the disappeared "witness" whom he'd dubbed *Miss Munch*...

...he'd been doing electrical repairs on a clothes dryer in the laundry at Pauline's refuge.

"How's your day going?" he had said to an owl-eyed woman who was wearing a dressing gown and bare feet. Her heels were the hue of radish skin.

She ignored him and tipped a basket of clothes into a washing machine.

"Good timing," he added. "I've just fixed it."

She set the wash cycle as if he wasn't there. Joe thought that maybe she was deaf, or that he was being a pain in the arse, and tried not to notice a couple of coin-sized bald patches on her scalp.

Pauline told him later in her office over a cup of tea that the woman could hear a pin drop, which was seriously unsettling for her in noisy places, and that her hair loss was due to psychological trauma diagnosed by a charming police force psychologist who had visited the refuge doing *research*.

Dr Ross Fellows, Joe learned, had focussed his attention on the woman like some kids put sunlight on ants with magnifying glasses. Fellows also befriended a second woman named Tracy Jarvis.

Pauline added that Fellows was attracted to Tracy because she was a heroin addict trying to get clean. Tracy had escaped nasty afflictions such as HIV and hepatitis so she wasn't a disease risk at close quarters. But what attracted Fellows most was the fact that Tracy had two pretty daughters aged nine and ten.

Tracy, however, was wary of men – that's why she and her daughters were living in a refuge after all. But when a gentleman from the police child protection unit invited her and her girls to the Wonderland Fun Park – and offered to take another woman from the refuge as a companion and chaperone – Tracy was in.

"This happened before I took the job as manager here," Pauline had said, topping up Joe's teacup. "We've tightened the rules now."

"What happened at Wonderland?" Joe had asked.

*

Ahead on the motorway, an electronic billboard loomed. Into Joe's skull popped a word, with many interesting branches, that he'd been discussing with his teacher and fellow students in literacy class: coincidence.

On the enlarging billboard, moving pictures showed laughing kids in swimwear racing down a waterslide. Giant words blazed: *Wonderland Fun Park – Family Day Special Today! Take Next Exit.*

As Joe passed by the sign, he used the van's cruise control button to set the accelerator at the speed limit, and let his mind's eye rove again…

…after leaving Wonderland, Pauline said that Fellows took the women and girls to a nearby town for a slap-up Chinese dinner.

After dinner, his car wouldn't start. The children were falling asleep. His generosity overflowed into an invitation to spend the night at a motel; this would be his shout too. They deserved spoiling after all the horrors they had been through before coming to the refuge.

The two women and girls could share a family room; he would take a separate room.

After Tracy had sipped a night-cap of Irish cream whiskey on ice that Fellows brought to her door after dinner, and with her girls tucked beside her in a comfortable bed, Tracy fell deeply asleep.

She woke at dawn's light with her daughters snug beside her. Like Tracy, the girls had gone to sleep wearing their underpants and T-shirts because they'd brought no pyjamas for the unplanned overnight stay. Tracy felt tender between her legs when she climbed out of bed and walked. She put it down to bumpy rides on the waterslide. Then her youngest daughter complained of having a sore "private". The child's vagina was inflamed. When she confronted Fellows, he told her to pull up the right sleeve of her long-sleeved T-shirt.

Tracy found a pockmark and a bruise on the big vein in the crook of her arm. Tracy knew a needle mark well enough.

Fellows assured her that traces of heroin would be found in her blood if a test was done, and Valium would be found in her daughters' blood. He reminded her that such a discovery would not go down well with the women's refuge, or child welfare authorities.

He added that in the early hours of the morning, while he had been smoking a cigarette on the veranda in front of his motel room, he had seen a strange man leave Tracy's room. And he would sign a police statement to that effect if asked.

This accusation about the stranger caused Tracy to seek the counsel of her travelling companion who was sitting on a bench on the motel veranda smoking one of Fellows' cigarettes.

Tracy told her friend that she suspected that Fellows had drugged and sexually abused both her and her daughters.

The woman had responded by puffing smoke and informing Tracy that she was speaking like a mad person. The chaperone said that she would provide an alibi for Fellows by swearing that she and the psychologist had spent the entire night together in his room, and that they had slept in separate beds. She was a light sleeper who woke at the merest sound, and Fellows had never left the room. Furthermore, she would sign a statement that Tracy was a guilt-ridden junkie who had confessed to her, at the refuge, that on more than one occasion she had drugged her daughters and sold them to men for sex in exchange for drugs and money.

The horror and powerlessness that Tracy felt had plunged her into mind-bending confusion, followed by a bout of clinical depression that disabled her for months inside Polaris House. But guilt and self-loathing weren't Tracy's alone; they chewed on the psyche of the other woman, and when the blackness eventually fell away from Tracy's mind, the other woman offered to support Tracy's drug and rape story if she went to the police. Tracy had then gone to the refuge's new manager, Pauline, for help.

Fellows soon faced sexual assault charges which he vehemently denied. Where was the evidence, he said? The allegations related to an event that supposedly occurred almost six months previously. The young girls had no experiences to recount, and there was no DNA proof that he had assaulted anyone. The case turned on the hearsay of two women: one a mother with a long history of drug abuse and mental illness; the other a woman who'd been diagnosed with a serious psychiatric disorder.

*

In the humming Firefly, Pauline stirred and opened her eyes.

"Pauls," said Joe. "Sorry if I'm disturbing you. What's the name for Miss Munch's illness?"

"Munchhausen's by proxy, Joe. It means that you hurt another person in order to get attention for yourself."

"Ta," he said.

Yes, thought Joe. Miss Munch got attention for herself from Tracy's trauma all right. Miss Munch became the star witness who could bring Fellows down. But then she disappeared, and all charges against Fellows were dropped.

Fellows' punishment had been a stint on workforce probation after the initial allegations, with an instruction from his superiors not to get so close to the women he met in his professional capacity. Now he was back helping to chase down sex offenders who preyed on children over the internet.

19 - PARADISE

THE COASTAL town of Hartlett was mostly a holiday and retirement community. Gouged from low hills and surrounded by dairy farms and timber plantations, it straddled the Pacific Highway which doubled as the main street.

"Dry as a dead dingo's donger out there," Joe concluded, blinking into a brutal, mid-afternoon sun. He motored past yellow grass in front of cottages made of weatherboard walls and shimmering corrugated iron rooves, others from bricks and tiles.

The residences gave way to shoebox-shaped brick and glass shops. The concrete footpaths were scattered with shufflers wearing wide-brimmed hats and sunglasses. Tongues drooped from the mouths of dogs. Pauline used an e-map on a tablet to direct Joe to their ultimate destination.

"Take the next left," she said. "The beach road."

Joe took in the sprawl of boxy houses on the flat, treeless bitumen trail to the sea. "These places...it's like the owners chuck their building plans into the council, and the council says, *cheers for the fees, we're off to the pub, whack up what you like.*"

"I expected absolute seafront, him being a doctor," said Lennie, rising from the armchair. He stepped through the van, palming off the walls for balance. He grabbed Rawcus's rod between the headrests of the front seats and peered through the windscreen.

"It's an academic title," Pauline explained. "He's not a medical doctor. Most academics don't use the moniker outside of uni. Milo has a doctorate too."

"Shit. He's probably not even a real psychologist," said Lennie. "I mean, anyone can build a website and fake a profile on Facebook and Wikipedia, you can pay people to beef it up. Hell, I might become a professor, hey?"

"What of?" said Pauline.

"I'm seeing stars."

"OK," said Pauline, nodding. She drew quote marks in the air with her fingers. "Leonard Larson, Professor of Particle Physics and Astronomy."

"Sir Leonard has a ring to it. Might as well grab a knighthood while I'm at it. Buy a bowtie. Tell people I'm a billionaire. As long as you don't owe people money, and say you live in the Bahamas, most people never question that shit."

"In a few years, you'll be embedded in the Establishment."

"Concreted in."

Joe shook his head. "Any chance you two can focus on Fellows?"

Pauline phoned TC and said that Carol should drive to the opposite end of town and await instructions. Lennie and Joe would do a recce inside the property first – if Fellows hadn't arrived. If he had arrived, they'd need to execute their Plan B to lure him outside. In any event, it was important, she reminded them, that Carol and TC turn up after dark so they could exploit the light and have the best chance of persuading Fellows that TC was a schoolgirl. Sundown was still hours away.

Joe reached a T-junction and turned left onto the beachfront road. There was no surf in Hartlett – it was a fishing, swimming, and wading place. A browned-off grass strip sat between the road and the white sand. The sea beyond was navy blue and a gentle offshore wind gave the seagull-peppered surface a rippled effect that Joe liked a lot. He thought about how in a few days, he and Lennie would be sailing aboard their little yacht *Flamingo Sky* – if today's mission didn't go arse up.

The doctor's backstreet was populated by mostly single-story, flat-roofed dwellings clad with faded weatherboard planks or paint-peeling fibre-cement sheets. They had straight-in drive-ways and patchy expanses of grey sand and dry lawn out front. The buildings were separated by head-high fences made mostly of metal sheets in shades of brown or dull green.

"Poor bugger," said Joe, looking up as they passed under-neath a dead possum dangling from a power line.

"A lot of imagination has gone into this architecture," Lennie observed.

Pauline frowned. "Not everyone can afford Palm Beach with a pool, Lennie."

"Fair point. But a lick of colour wouldn't break the bank."

Pauline pointed through her side window. "That's his place."

"Wow!" said Lennie.

Joe slowed to a crawl. No vehicles were visible in the driveway, so he stopped and reversed, pulling up in front of Fellows' house.

The building reminded him of a couple of shoeboxes arranged into an L-shape. The short side of the L faced the street. The long, left side of the L ran beside a brown metal fence. A grey gravel driveway stretched down the right side of the building.

Lennie leaned further into the Firefly's cabin and studied the house through Pauline's window. He couldn't see a front door from the street and figured it must be hidden somewhere on the inside corner of the L, which was handy for their Plan A. Inserted in the street-front wall of the L were two square windows.

"Well, I believe we underestimated our man," said Lennie, impressed by the blue walls, yellow window frames, and red gutters. The skin on the back of his neck tingled. The entire house began radiating.

"How did we do that?" said Joe.

"Howard Arkley," Lennie blurted. "He's got himself a Howard Arkley house. Not the finest example, clad in that fibrecement, but it's still a H-A."

"See what you mean," said Joe, who knew Arkley's psychedelic paintings of Australian box houses of the 1960s and 1970s from a coffee table book that Lennie gave him for his birthday a few years back. The book came wrapped with a couple of tabs of LSD. Inside Joe's skull, the cover image of Arkley's *Carnival of Suburbia* resurrected itself in glorious technicolor.

Lennie felt an otherworldly force fiddling with a dimmer dial, toning down then brightening the hues of the house. Words floated into his skull: "tomato-red", "buttercup-yellow", "Hindu-blue".

He said, "It's like the house knows we're coming. It's calling us even."

Joe sensed Lennie was drifting off the dry Hartlett turf; it was Joe's job to bring him back to earth.

"Can't see any external cameras," said Joe.

Lennie scratched his head. "You sure we have the right place, Pauls? I expected better security."

"Check. This is the address he gave Carol."

Joe said, "Could be a setup."

Lennie curled his lips. "Mm. Let's park at the end of the street, mate, next to that bushland." He pointed. "How about in the shade under that tree? And keep her nose-out, so if Fellows turns up, Pauls can spot him and phone us."

As Joe manoeuvred the van, Lennie moved back to the armchair and swapped his black T-shirt for a red polo shirt. He put a matching red baseball cap on his skull.

"Can you chuck us a couple of those business cards from the glovebox, please Pauls?"

Pauline glanced at the cards. "Very impressive. *Bob Peters. Managing Director. Bolt Electrical.*"

"Thanks," said Lennie. He put them in the front pocket of his polo shirt.

Pauline scanned the street. "Like a ghost town. No-one out."

Joe wound down his window. "Phew! You could fry eggs on the rocks out there." He tapped the button on the window riser.

"Good for us," said Lennie, tapping the wooden Jack in his pocket. He tossed Joe an XXXL-size red polo shirt and matching cap.

Lennie picked up the backpack with Tremlett's pistol inside it. He checked that it also contained house keys; battery-powered, micro-cameras; wire crimps and cutters; and other electrician's tools. He climbed out and threw the sliding door shut.

Joe was waiting, holding a battery-powered drill, a pair of vehicle registration plates, and the white magnetic sheets that disguised the Firefly for the Galaxy Motel operation.

Joe applied the sheets. Lennie switched the number plates.

"Let's have a test run," said Lennie, removing his cap and wiping sweat off his brow. He tapped a knuckle on his head.

"Huh?" said Joe.

"You're the householder," said Lennie. "I'm the friendly caller at your door." Lennie knocked on his head again.

Joe grunted, "What do you want? I'm fuckin' busy bakin' a cake."

Lennie bowed. "Good afternoon, sir. I'm Bob Peters from Bolt Electrical. We received a call-out to this address. I believe you have problems with a safety switch that you can't re-set?"

"Listen, Bob. I'll re-set ya face if ya don't get ya fat arse off my property."

"I'm very sorry, Mr Bakewell. Head office must have given me the wrong address."

Joe tilted his cap up, wiped sweat, and nodded. "Not bad...let's get crackin' before the real prick shows up."

Joe as the apprentice carried the backpack of tools and spy devices over his shoulder. His managing director carried a clipboard tucked under an arm and a pen behind his right ear, given that his left was no good for carrying pencils because a vital chunk had been clipped away by a pair of pliers wielded by an Enoka brother in prison several years ago.

The gravel on the driveway crunched under their feet, so loudly that Lennie wondered if the loose stones were Fellows' early-warning alarm. They turned into the inner corner of the L-shaped building.

A red door sat proud in the long side of the blue-walled L, hidden from the street. A head-high-plus, metal-sheet fence bordered the outer edge of the driveway, blocking the neighbour's view of the door.

Lennie scanned the walls. "Can't see any CCTV."

"Smart," said Joe, thinking how security cameras were a dead-set giveaway to would-be thieves that there was good shit inside.

Lennie stepped to the door and tapped a knuckle on the wood panel. He waited. Listened. Tapped some more. Banged with a fist.

"Let's get to it," said Joe.

"What if someone's flaked out hugging a bottle of rum?"

"Either way, there won't be any resistance."

Lennie smiled and stooped to read the brand on the door furniture. "Wedlock. How romantic."

Joe unzipped his backpack and pulled out two pairs of flesh-coloured surgical gloves. They put them on.

Joe extracted a large metal ring, with dozens of keys on it, that had fallen off the back of a truck owned by a locksmith who hated receipts but loved premium-grade Mars Grass. He fanned through the bunched families of master keys which covered every leading brand of doorlock known to modern man, so the locksmith claimed. The Wedlock family was tagged with orange key-heads. Joe handed the bunch to Lennie.

Thump!

"Shit!" hissed Lennie. "Someone's in there."

They listened. Silence. Lennie knocked again. No answer.

Joe put an ear to the door. "Might be a possum doing a break and enter. They're around."

"Fuck this," said Lennie. "We're losing time."

After a few attempts with the Wedlocks, Lennie pushed the door open. "Hello!" he called into the house. "Neighbourhood Watch, here. Your door was open. Everything OK?"

Silence.

They went inside and pulled the door shut.

"Confident bugger," said Joe, surveying the sitting room. "Still no cameras. Very slack approach to security for a man in his position."

"Must think he's invincible after escaping the noose with Tracy and her girls," said Lennie.

"And Miss Munch."

Joe sneezed.

Lennie froze.

"Could have sensors under the carpet," said Lennie, eyeing the eggshell-coloured pile near his feet looking for lumps. "Those apps that shoot alerts to your phone are catching on."

"Let's not paralyse ourselves," said Joe.

Lennie scanned the ceilings and walls. "This whole fucking place might be booby-trapped."

Joe reached into the backpack and pulled out the pistol. "If he turns up before we've done our business, he can say hi to Mr Glock. A lot of options will open up from there."

"This is disturbing," said Lennie, lifting off the floor a window-fronted envelope marked with a water company logo. "The bill's for this address, but who the hell is *Hector Marlowe?*"

"Reckon he keeps this place in a fake name?"

"Could borrow it off a friend." Joe pulled a tissue from his pocket and wiped his dripping nose. "Or maybe he smelled a rat and gave Carol a fake address."

"Lot of balls in the air now," said Lennie. "Gawd. We might just get pictures of some geriatrics changing each other's nappies tonight."

"Whadda we do?"

"Crack on, I reckon."

The L-shaped layout made exploration easy.

The square sitting room had cream-coloured carpet and walls. It was furnished with an oatmeal-coloured, three-seater sofa backed against the driveway-side wall. A glass-topped coffee table sat in front of the sofa. At either end of the table were matching armchairs. All the seating was aimed at a widescreen TV perched upon a low bench against the wall directly opposite the front door.

A single ceiling light hung on a chrome rod with three, frosted-glass shades.

Joe stepped to the left side of the sitting room and faced a wall into which two, side-by-side doors were built.

He quick-stepped through the right-side doorway: the room contained two single beds, matching bedside tables with reading lamps, and floor-to-ceiling, built-in wardrobes with sliding mir-rored doors. Inside the wardrobes, pillows, blankets, and sheets were stacked on shelves. Very tidy, thought Joe, in an old person's way. No incontinence nappies that he could see.

Lennie had turned to the right side of the sitting room under a crescent-shaped arch into the kitchen. The lino floor was of a hue that reminded him of boiled cauliflower and cheddar cheese soup. A stainless-steel sink and draining board were set into a bench under a net-curtained window that overlooked the driveway. On the opposite wall, a standalone, top-opening freezer abutted a white fridge that stood beside a grey Formica-topped workbench which encased an electric cooker. In the middle of the room, a wooden table was surrounded by half a dozen country-kitchen chairs. The air smelled of bleach. Very tidy, thought Lennie, like a doctor's surgery.

Joe stepped back into the sitting area and entered the second bedroom that was closest to the driveway: a double bed stood in the middle of the room, its headboard propped against the wall it shared with the bedroom next door. On the left side of the room, there was a built-in wardrobe. Joe rolled aside the mirrored doors: men's clothes hung from wire hangers on a rail. The shirts, trousers, and jackets didn't look like old-aged pensioners' clobber. One dark suit was labelled Hugo Boss. Joe checked the pockets. Empty.

Like the sleeping room next door, the double bedroom had a small square window facing the street that was dressed with closed net curtains and a closed Venetian blind.

Joe joined Lennie as he was inspecting the bathroom connected to the kitchen at the back of the house. The toilet, built-in bathtub, and separate glass-screen shower were standard-issue but spotless.

"Tidy fucker," said Joe. "Not a photo in sight. Found a clue, though. There's a suit that belongs to a guy called Hugo Boss."

"Very funny," said Lennie.

He opened a laundry cupboard. "Well, hello old friends!"

He eyed a blue bottle of household bleach; a green bottle of isopropyl alcohol; a stainless steel measuring jug; and a pair of thick, red rubber gloves. A respirator sat on the shelf below.

"Do you think Hugo Boss is the type to cook up homemade chloroform?" said Lennie.

"Maybe he has trouble sleeping."

Lennie closed the cupboard and opened a door that led into the laundry behind the bathroom. He un-slotted three bolts on another door, pulled it open, and flipped the catch on a flywire-screen door which led down steps to a brick-paved area, shaded by an awning made of metal sheets atop steel poles. The only thing under the covered space was a waterproof-hooded barbeque on wheels. Beyond the paving was a treeless patchwork of sand and brown grass.

"Nice," said Lennie.

"Paradise," said Joe.

They stepped inside, rebolted the door, and returned to the sitting room.

"Can you smell that?" said Lennie.

"What?"

"Death. Like a morgue."

"Have you taken one of TC's lollies?"

"I'm serious."

"I can't smell a thing. But I'm getting a cold, or I'm allergic to something in here."

"Yeah. Evil most likely. Did you count the lightbulbs?"

"Seventeen if we include the front and back porch lights."

Lennie stepped into the kitchen and returned with a chair which he placed under the sitting room ceiling light. He climbed up and removed one of the lampshades. "He's using screw-ins. Take this sampler. Make sure you get the low watt bulbs."

"How long have I been your apprentice?"

"Sorry, mate. He's close. Feels like I'm sitting on a razor."

"Back in a flash."

Lennie sniffed the air. He told himself to keep a lid on his imagination, but the pot was boiling and the cover was hopping. The stink of disinfectant and decomposing flesh triggered a visual recall of the rat their neighbour's deaf, one-eyed black cat, Bruce, had been de-boning when Tremlett's gang hit.

Lennie scoured the sitting room for a place to rig one of his micro-cameras which had memory cards and batteries that could record about four hours of video. But the furnishings were sparse, the light fittings minimal, and there was no art on the walls to distract the eye either. The only helpful thing was the cream colour of the walls.

Lennie extracted from the backpack a matchbox-sized camera with an off-white shell. Its black eye was about the same size as one of Rawcus's, prompting Lennie to wonder how the little bloke was feeling. He dragged the kitchen chair to a corner of the sitting room, peeled the sticky-back protector off the shell, and clicked the on-switch. He climbed the chair and stuck the spyware in a corner where the ceiling met the wall. He stepped down and examined his installation. Not great, but not bad. What's the downside if Fellows finds it?

Plenty, he acknowledged, if he trapped Carol and TC in here. As well as being a paedophile rapist, the braggart doctor might be a witness killer. What would he do with that chloroform? The ceiling creaked. Shit! Was someone walking up there? He pulled the Glock from the backpack and flicked the safety off. There was a manhole in the ceiling above the TV and smudged fingerprints on the paintwork around the cover. He dragged the chair underneath the hole. Was the ugly smell coming from up there?

"What the fuck?" said Joe, stepping in and closing the door. He was carrying a plastic shopping bag containing the new globes.

"Inside the roof," said Lennie, pointing the gun at the manhole. "It sounds like walking."

Joe listened. There was a creak. "Sun's going down. The tin roof's cooling."

Lennie lowered the weapon. "This place is alive."

"We need to move it," said Joe. He sneezed.

Lennie put mini-cams in each bedroom and the kitchen. Joe changed all the bulbs in the house to the low watt units.

In the sitting room, Lennie bent up slightly the bottom blade of the Venetian blind in the window that overlooked the driveway.

"Spyhole for later," he said. "We can use that fisheye lens. OK, quick check and we're out of here."

In the double bedroom, while testing the new bulbs, Lennie looked at his grainy image in the wardrobe mirror. "Got me buggered why shops light fitting rooms like dentist surgeries? TC might get away with it in the romantic glow of these low watters."

"You know what I don't get about this place?" said Joe.

"His cutting edge interior design?"

"Close...there's a room missing, or a bit of one."

"What room?"

"If you're in a helicopter, this house is shaped like you're looking down on the letter L. Yeah?"

"And?"

"Well, we've just been moving up and down one long corridor really. Part of the short side of the L is missing. Not on the outside. Just on the inside."

Lennie rubbed in his chin, nodding at the mirrored door of the built-in wardrobe. "Gotcha."

They opened the sliding door, pushed aside the clothes on the hangers, and tapped the wall which emitted a hollow sound. That was to be expected. All the internal walls were clad with gyprock plasterboards over timber frames.

"Let's have a look outside," said Lennie. "But we'll tidy up first. Don't want to get busted with our gear everywhere."

After packing their equipment and stuffing the discarded bulb boxes in the backpack, they stood near the driveway inside the corner of the L.

Hidden from the street, they studied the double bedroom wall.

"You're right," said Lennie.

Joe nodded. "He's got a secret room in there."

Lennie's phone started bleating inside his jeans pocket.

"Yes, Pauls?"

"Incoming. Black four-wheel-drive. You've got thirty seconds tops."

20 - THE WOLF

"HE'S HERE," said Lennie, pivoting towards Joe. "We got everything?"

Joe's eyes popped. "Clipboard!" He scampered towards the open door.

Lennie whipped off his gloves and stuffed them in his back pocket, straightening his baseball cap to the sound of tyres crunching gravel.

Joe backed out of the front door, holding the backpack and the clipboard in front of his belly. He pulled the door shut and stripped off one glove, turning to see a black car rolling to a stop beside them.

Fellows flung open the driver's door and charged around the front of his vehicle in a blur of dark suit and white shirt, snatching his sunglasses off his face. "What the fuck are you arseholes doing?"

Joe slipped his gloved hand inside the backpack. He felt the pistol grip and flipped the safety off.

"Good afternoon," Lennie said to Fellows. "Electricians. We didn't think anyone was home. We were about to leave a card.

Received a call-out to this address. You have a safety switch that you can't re-set, I believe?'

Fellows looked from Lennie to Joe, and back to Lennie. "Wrong fucking address, pal."

"We're sorry," said Lennie. "Head office must have got its wires crossed."

"Comedian too, hey?" said Fellows, who looked at Joe who kept his hand inside the backpack. "Are you holding your dick in there, big boy?"

A dog started barking, hearty woofs, but muted. The three men turned to face the near-side back window of Fellows' car. A massive animal with a pointy head, black nose and stiff ears bounced against the glass, clunking it with gnashing teeth, smearing it with slobber in its fury.

"He's excited," said Lennie. "Or is it a she?"

"Hungry male," said Fellows.

"Enjoy the rest of your day," said Lennie, extending his right hand to shake Fellows'. "Sorry about the stuff-up with the address."

Fellows ignored Lennie's outstretched hand. "That your van at the end of the street under the tree?"

"Yup," said Lennie.

"Why are you hiding it up there?"

"Not hiding. Got an apprentice with us today. We did an outdoor job at the sports oval and she caught a bit of sunstroke. Bloody hot today. It's caused a few outages, which ain't bad for business to be honest."

"She cute?" said Fellows.

Lennie wondered if this was Mr Clever Dick psychologist engaging in clichéd banter with a couple of dumb tradesmen. But this wasn't the time to play clever back.

"She's better looking than him," said Lennie, nodding at Joe who smiled. Lennie shook his head ever so slightly at Joe, signalling "don't do it".

"I get it. You're both giving her a length," said Fellows. "Got a nice set-up in the back of the van, have you?"

"It's comfortable enough," said Lennie, wrestling the urge to dropkick Fellows in the nuts and shortcut this entire mission. "Anyway, we might see you another time."

"Not fucking likely," said Fellows. "But you better give me a card so I know where to get you."

Lennie handed Fellows a business card from his top pocket.

"Mr Big Time," said Fellows, reading the card. "Managing Director, hey? No wonder the apprentice is throwing herself on your cock."

Joe and Lennie walked side-by-side down the driveway. They turned left into the street and headed towards the van.

"Red," said Lennie, picturing the chart of the *F for Ethics Colour Scheme* by which they rated people's characters. "He could turn from orange to red very quickly."

Joe released the gun and pulled his hand from the backpack. "There's this much in it," he said, drawing a thumb and index finger so close there was barely a hair's breadth gap saving Fellows from a terminal ruling.

*

On the outskirts of Hartlett beside a bushland park, the five gathered inside the Firefly.

TC's face needed a touch-up because the heat had caused minor melting. With that done, the consensus was that *Donna* looked better than passable, especially as day was giving way to the night.

"We have a new variable. Two actually," said Lennie. "He turned up with a huge dog."

"It looked like a wolf," said Joe.

"And he's got a secret room," said Lennie, sketching a floor-plan of Fellows' house on a page of his A4 notebook. "We didn't get in there."

21 - NARNIA

FELLOWS STOOD at his kitchen bench and peeled cling-film from a long bone flecked with pink flesh and white fat. Holding the bone at arm's length, he carried it towards the back of his house.

He opened the flywire screen and tossed the limb clattering onto the brick paving. An Alsatian dog, chained to a pole by a leather collar, pounced, clapping its mighty teeth on the prize with a crack that caused the hairs on Fellows' neck to rise.

"Nourish yourself, Aslan," he said. "You'll need your strength tonight."

Fellows busied himself unpacking his car. He had plenty of fish and red meat; fruit and salad; and beer, spirits, and wine. He placed everything neatly in the kitchen.

Fellows wheeled his travel case into the double bedroom, and checked that his medicine kit was inside it and that nothing was spilled or broken.

Carol and Donna would be OK sharing the room with the single beds. He'd never had a problem with that arrangement. Sharing made both parent and offspring feel secure.

He would cook a barbeque of steaks and chicken kebabs and make a green salad tonight. And then they could watch a DVD. He'd purchased a fresh copy of *The Chronicles of Narnia: The Lion, the Witch and the Wardrobe* today. A twelve-year-old girl will like that movie, and so will her mum. That would relax them, he thought, like pre-meds in a hospital before surgery.

He was weary from the drive and hot from unpacking. He sat on the sofa and unbuttoned his shirt. Rest for a moment. He dozed...

Ping! A text from Carol. She and Donna were approaching the outskirts of Hartlett. They would be with him in about thirty minutes, if they didn't lose their way. Fellows looked out of the open front door. Shit! Night was falling.

Shit! He shouldn't have fallen asleep! He needed to check his own *Narnia* before they arrived.

Fellows strode into his bedroom and slid aside the mirrored door of the walk-in wardrobe. He took from his trouser pocket an electronic key and pressed a button. Click! A wall panel swung open into the vault he called *Narnia*.

What an achievement, he thought. He'd designed, built, and installed the door unassisted and it pleased him greatly. It comprised a full-thickness piece of wall, timber-framed and clad with gyprock so that it looked and sounded, if it was knocked upon, like every other wall in the house. The electronically-controlled, motor-driven hinges were his masterstroke. The seals were perfect.

Fellows stepped into the wardrobe then out into *Narnia*. Ceiling lights blinked on and illuminated the cube of window-less space.

Beside the wall to his left, a digital camera was mounted on a tripod. Next to the tripod were three floodlights attached to adjustable floor stands. A table was tucked into a far corner. Upon the table sat a flat-screen TV and a laptop computer. A flag-sized map of the world was attached to the wall above the table, with the cities and towns of many countries marked by pins with coloured heads. A blue pin was stuck in Monterrey, Mexico. Yellow in Manchester, England. Green in Cologne, Germany. Pink in Yokohama, Japan.

The pink pin made him think of raw fish. He'd never understood the Japanese obsession with it. But he did like some of the Japs bedroom furniture. So much so that he was a collector. A stuffed-cotton futon mattress was rolled and stacked by a wall.

Futons were paradoxically soft and firm, and Fellows loved a paradox. But mostly he liked the way futons could be shaped using his hands, knees, or feet into a range of robust contours. He dragged the futon into the middle of the room.

It was groundbreaking work, this research he was doing to improve his knowledge and skills as a psychologist advising the police force on what makes the minds tick of those who obtain gratification from the sexual exploitation of children. His colleagues wouldn't understand his methods, he knew that, but someone in his profession had to fearlessly explore what human beings were capable of. He was an astronaut travelling into the outer reaches of man's inner space. He glanced at a book he kept on his studio table.

He might even read *120 Days of Sodom* by Marquis de Sade someday. But the tome, from what he'd read so far, was narrow-mindedly anal. Moreover, reading textbooks, or novels, or fishing on the internet and screen-gazing to obtain knowledge was a tediously academic experience.

It was only by personally probing the boundaries of the human imagination, by going into the field, vulnerable and exposed in every way, by trekking the spectrum of both the physical and psychic worlds, that he could properly perform his job. He was already more expert than any of his timid colleagues. Staying at the cutting edge of his craft necessitated the contact of his flesh *upon* flesh. It was not about mind over matter, it was about mind *and* matter. Only thus could he truly know how the human psyche works in this realm.

Fellows dropped to his knees in front of the sausage-rolled futon and draped his arms over it. No, that didn't feel right. He slipped the ties on the futon and laid it flat. Then he dragged up one end to meet the other, sandwiching the halves. He laid belly-first into the futon's curve, his knees on the carpet, and turned his head to one side to breathe. That position was gold. He could use a pillow too, tuck it under their knees to adjust their hips and buttocks if necessary.

He stood and dusted flecks of carpet off his trousers. He reached inside his jacket pocket and extracted a small plastic bag.

He peeled its seal apart and licked the tip of his little finger, dipping it into the white crystals. Fellows put the finger to his tongue; bitterness fizzed upon his tastebuds. Amphetamines were not his first choice. But his cocaine supply had dried up this week, so tonight was going to be a rockier and less predictable ride than he'd desired. He had to stay uber alert. Because his guests would be going the other way. Unconsciousness was a kindness he would show them.

In most of his experiments of the imagination, his subjects were anaesthetised and as pliable as dolls – and this thoughtful subtlety separated him from the truly depraved. It was in fact him, the intrepid adventurer Dr Ross Fellows, PhD, who risked his sanity and humanity by staying awake inside this laboratory when he pushed the button on what he called *The Flipside*. His subjects would simply wake in the morning in their beds, unaware of where they had been. If anything, they would recall a dream.

OK, he thought, there'd been the odd slip-up. Things had gone awry with Tracy and that terrible woman with Munchausen's by proxy and, he felt sure, bipolar disorder. But that's what happens when you go to the boundaries of things: accidents happen. He had asked for trouble by going off-piste to that bloody motel after the day at Wonderland. Anyway, the psycho with Munchausen's wouldn't be giving him any more trouble, that's for sure.

The doctor licked his fingers and stuck them in the bag. He sniffed and licked. And sniffed and licked. What's that noise? Barking. Outside. Shit!

Quick! He trotted through the house to the backdoor, threw it open and commanded: "Heel!"

The ex-police dog he'd named Aslan followed him through the house and the wardrobe into *Narnia*.

"Sit," said Fellows, and the dog did.

My mask, my mask, he thought, don't forget that. He'd need that tonight. Where was it? Oh yes, on the wall-side table, in the wooden box. He took from the box a flesh-coloured leather facemask with eyeholes. He took his spectacles off, placed them on the table, and put the mask on, fixing it in place with a leather cord that he tied at the back of his head. He looked into a floor-to-ceiling wall mirror. The mask covered his cheekbones, his forehead, and the bridge of his nose down to its tip. He didn't need his spectacles to see the red, almond-shaped spot between the eyes, *the third eye* as the Hindus called it. For a moment, he felt he was inside the mind of the mask's donor.

He stuck his finger in the amphetamine bag and licked it clean. There were two more jobs.

He needed more space to work with tonight. Fellows pushed along the floor a cardboard box stamped as containing 1,000 blank memory cards, each card with 100GB of capacity. They could hold 30 to 40 hours of video each, and they were as small as postage stamps. He kicked the box under the table.

The master videos which he created were required for re-search − for playback and review. Absolutely appropriate, he reassured himself, for how could he take proper academic notes while he was in the thick of the action? Of course, he must have the videos − for post-analysis.

And so what if he ran off a few extra copies and sent them to the towns and cities pinned on his world map? Research costs money, and this was private research he was doing with no government funding. He had a good customer base now, one it had taken several years to build. Sending a few memory cards through the post, or via the plethora of courier companies that internet shopping had spawned, was a lot safer than distributing live online these days. Ha. He should know − he worked for the police! He licked his finger. Repowered.

Fellows smiled, an idea flowered, its petals unfolded: he would do an interview – with himself.

"So Dr Fellows," said Fellows, "packaging is very important in your line of work. How do you do it?"

"That's a trade secret, Dr Fellows."

"You're among friends."

"I don't trust myself."

"Ha. Knowing you, I'm sure it's clever."

"You're a charmer. Truth is, I recently purchased a compact commercial printing and packaging machine from China. What a fabulous industrial economy that is. I mean, the quality and value alone..."

"Can we stick to the point, doctor?"

"You can talk."

"You're the one being interviewed."

"OK. OK. Well, this equipment enables me to open the real manufacturers' sealed memory cards, download my movies onto them, and then use the machine to insert the loaded cards into brand-new, professional packets under the original brand."

"Wow. That's a stroke of genius."

"You're too kind, Dr Fellows. But no, I think the genius is adding a T-shirt or a paperback book, or another item when I post it, to make it look like a genuine gift to a friend."

Ping! Fellows plucked his phone from his pocket. Carol! On approach!

He took off the mask. "Time! Time!" he huffed.

One last job. He opened a desk drawer and extracted a snub-nosed revolver. He checked that the Ruger was loaded, and put it back. Firearms were as scary as snakes and a last resort, but in his business, he'd met psychos who couldn't be reasoned with. And you never knew when a lunatic might knock, even when you hide your world under the pseudonym, *Hector Marlowe*. Or *Will Carter*, or...

"Damn," he muttered. He opened the drawer below the gun. The inflatable doll of a child was still in its packaging. Got to burn that, he told himself. Why the hell did *Hector Marlowe* ever buy that from his coke dealer? Drunk and wired to the eyeballs at the time, that's why! It was research, Marlowe argued. That fucking Uber driver and his Guardian newspaper, Fellows cursed. The driver's words rang: *I could swear I've seen you on the news...you're going to be famous one day, sir.*

"Like fuck I'll be in the news," Fellows muttered.

The dog whined. Fellows glanced at Aslan: "Stay. Good boy. Quiet! Sit!"

The dog growled. It didn't sit.

*

Fellows stepped from the wardrobe into his bedroom and pressed the electronic key. The door drew shut, leaving him in gloom. He backed against a wall and used it as a guide to slide to the doorframe where he felt for a light switch. He flipped it.

Strange, he thought, the overhead light was very dim, jaundiced. He stepped to the bedside table and turned the lamp on. It added little. He blamed the new amphetamines for his unusually mellow perspective. There was a knock at his front door.

Carol was standing alone on the doorstep when he opened it. A bolt of anger flashed through him; he tried to quell it.

"Where's Donna?" he said.

"We had a bit of a row."

"But she's here?"

"She won't get out of the car. Best to leave her to it for a bit. You know how kids are."

"Of course. Please, come in. Do you have luggage?"

"I'll get it in a moment. When she's had time to calm down."

"You must need a drink, after that drive. And the clash of the titans by the sound of it."

Carol followed him into the kitchen. "White wine if you have it. Anything cold and not too sweet."

"Please," he said, motioning for Carol to take a seat at the kitchen table.

He opened the fridge and extracted a bottle of chardonnay. He put it on the nearest benchtop and reached into a cupboard for a glass.

Carol glanced back into the sitting room. "Where's your daughter? Helen?"

"Oh, yes. I'm sorry," he said. "She's sick I'm afraid. She came down with a tummy bug today and her mother insisted she wasn't well enough to come away with me. I hope you are not too disappointed. It was very last minute, and I didn't see the point of upsetting your weekend as well."

"That is a shame, Will. Oh well, Donna will be disappointed, but there you go. The weather reports for the weekend are good. Plenty of sun, so it should be nice for swimming."

"Yes, good for sunbathing," he said.

He handed her a glass of wine. He mixed himself brown rum with ginger beer on ice in a tumbler. He extended his glass towards hers. They clinked.

"Cheers," he said. His spine trilled with anticipation. How long will Donna be sulking in the car?

"Carol, I'm sorry," he said. "But the lighting in this room. Does everything seem a little dim to you?"

"No. It's fine. Why?"

A knock at the door. Carol moved to stand, but in a half-hearted way.

"No. Let me, please." Fellows put his tumbler on the kitchen table and stepped into the sitting room towards the door.

With Fellows out of sight, Carol tipped half her glass of wine down the sink.

Approaching the front door, Fellows constructed his most sincere smile, and tapped his jacket pocket searching for his spectacles so he could get a decent look at Donna. Shit! He'd left them in *Narnia* in his rush. Oh well, they were just for reading and in-close work; he could see well enough for now. He opened the door to a schoolgirl standing at the bottom of the steps. She was looking at her feet, rubbing together the toes of her black, lace-up shoes. One white sock was down; her skinny arms dangled by her side; her shoulder-length hair fell about her face.

"Hi, Donna. I'm Ro...." Fellows shook his head. "Will. I'm Will."

"Hi," she whispered, then chewed gum.

"Please, come in."

Fellows studied this unusual girl. She was pretty alright, from what he could see of her face underneath her cascade of hair. She was flat-chested and narrow hipped and that was good. The photo Carol had sent him via *LovingLife.com* had looked different somehow. Never mind; she was here now. Donna stepped into the sitting room, head down. He liked shy girls. In time, he might also meet Donna's friends from school. What wasn't there to love about life, he thought, and all its possibilities?

TC scanned the room and turned an eye to the archway that led to the kitchen. Carol, seated at the kitchen table, was withdrawing her hand from over a glass of brown drink. She raised a thumb at TC.

At the heavy clunk of the front door lock, her hands began shaking. She looked at her wristwatch...

22 - LOLLIES

"IT SHOULD be kicking in about now," said Lennie, who slouched in the armchair in the Firefly and fiddled with a Rubik's Snake.

Pauline spied on Fellows' house from the front seat using binoculars. "I'm still not sure I agree with your approach."

Lennie clicked the Rubik's Snake into a cat shape. "That horse has bolted now, Pauls".

Joe lifted a hand off the steering wheel and plucked a chunky chip from a takeaway fish and chip box that was sitting in his lap. "Nothin like a good look inside yourself. Like a breath of fresh air."

Joe chewed. A cool sea breeze wafted through his open window and jostled his hair.

Lennie held up to the rays of an internal ceiling light a glass jar that glowed green from the tinted sugar cubes inside it.

He said, "Now, we thought this stuff was going to play to our advantage because we'd know what entered his brain while he didn't, and our feet would be on the ground while his wouldn't."

Pauline placed the binoculars in her lap and swivelled to face Lennie. "Where are you going with this, love?"

"Look, he's got the hidden room in his house that's a black hole to us, and the mad dog. There could be more surprises, especially when he starts seeing things that we can't. So the more I think about it, the more I reckon we should go in there with all possible eyes open, if you get my drift."

"Joe?" said Pauline.

Joe wiped his lips with a paper napkin. "Lennie drops half a cube, I drop the other. We match Fellows' one cube."

"Seriously?" said Pauline, rolling her eyes.

Lennie said, "How about I take one cube? Joe takes none. We match Fellows' one cube."

"My advice," Pauline said, "is that you just don't go there. It's not only your lives you're playing with tonight. Carol and TC are in that mad Howard Arkley house as you call it."

"Fair enough, Pauls," said Joe. He placed the napkin in the takeaway box and closed the lid.

Lennie nodded. He put the jar of LSD-infused sugar cubes in a drawer of the wall cabinet. "Let's get kitted up," he said.

He checked that he had a Jack inside the front pocket of his black jeans. Then he reached into a duffle bag at his feet and extracted a sheer black stocking and a pair of kid-leather black gloves. He was already dressed in black, calf-length boots and a skin-hugging, long-sleeved black shirt. He pulled the open end of the stocking over his skull, tugging it down until his entire head was snugly inside and the excess was ringed around the neck of his shirt. Then he pulled on the gloves.

Joe stared at his friend, who looked almost not-there. If there was such a thing as a human shadow, Lennie was it.

"Eyes," said Joe. "You need eye holes."

"Na," said Lennie, his sight adjusting to the light penetrating the sheer fabric. "I'll be fine. I'm tuning in."

Joe turned to face Pauline. She opened a box of face paints and stuck her fingers into the red pot. She smeared it thickly upon Joe's face and neck, pushing it all the way to the hairline of his tangled mop of naturally red-orange locks. She wiped her fingers clean on a rag, then dipped them in the pot of orange. She blended orange waves into the red. She finished the job with strands of gaslight blue running diagonally from a temple across an eye and nose onto a cheek, ending under Joe's jaw.

"Faark," said Lennie. "Your whole head's on fire."

"Duffle bag, mate," Joe said to Lennie. "I'll put the rest of my clobber on by the side of the van. No room to swing a cat in here."

Lennie handed Joe the bag, then turned to Pauline. "*Scary Monsters*, Pauls, if you don't mind. So we can get in the groove. About halfway in."

She slipped a CD into the music player. David Bowie let fly: *...She opened strange doors that we'd never close again...*

The side door of the van flew open. Lennie looked out and marvelled at the flaming head that floated in the dark in front of him.

Against the moonless sky, he found it hard to see the rest of Joe, who was wearing black track pants tucked into black biker boots, a black long-sleeved top, and matching gloves. The darkness was only disrupted by the mustard glow of a distant streetlamp.

"Here," said Lennie, stepping down onto the grass. He handed Joe a pair of latex gloves. "You know what boy scouts say."

"Don't get in the tent with Mr Wolf?" Joe tucked the back-up gloves in his track pants pocket.

Singing wafted: *Scary monsters, super creeps... Keep me running, running scared...*

A phone pinged. Pauline read the text and flashed a thumbs-up. Carol had got the sugar cube into Fellows somehow. The party was swinging. If the micro-cameras were working OK, they would soon have the video they were after of Dr Ross Fellows, PhD, trying to drug and rape an underage girl and her mother, or at least evidence enough to throw his reputation into melt-down and give the official hounds of law enforcement reason to tear Fellows' secret life apart.

"Now for the icing on the cake," said Lennie, standing by the side of the van. He tucked Tremlett's black pistol in the front waistband of his jeans and flinched at the shock of cold steel on his tummy.

"After you," said the flaming head to the shadow, who slipped a fisheye lens into the front pocket of his black jeans.

23 - THE THIRD EYE

THE REDHEAD and shadow stepped as silently as they could along the gravel driveway.

"Shit," Joe whispered as they saw the front door. "We missed the porchlight bulb."

"I've got a hunch that'll work in our favour," said Lennie, reckoning that some serious wattage, instead of low, would bring out the best in Joe's face.

They tiptoed to the sitting room window and looked through the slit between the bottom of the sill and the Venetians that Lennie had created earlier. Joe's eyes popped wide open; Lennie lifted his stocking mask to his brow: Fellows was naked, standing just inside the window with his pink bum pointing at them.

Lennie pulled the fisheye magnifier from his pocket and placed it gently against the window-glass. The sitting room expanded in the viewfinder.

Inside the warped world, on the big TV screen against the far wall, a lion was fighting a wolf. Standing beside the TV, TC was gyrating slowly, arms up like a stripper, circling. He'd cast off his schoolgirl's tunic and was dressed in the short-sleeved white shirt with the buttons undone over his flat chest, nipples flashing. His white underpants were tugged up at the back and wedged into his bum-crack. He remained shod in his black lace-up shoes and white calf-length socks.

Lennie turned the fisheye to his left: Carol was slouched on one of the single armchairs, her head tilted back and her eyes apparently closed, still wearing most of her sleeveless frock, but a shoulder strap had fallen and the frock's hem was rucked up to her bellybutton. Lennie handed the fisheye to Joe.

"Do you think Carol's foxing?" Lennie whispered.

"She looks out like a light. Maybe he hit her with the chloroform."

Lennie took the fisheye back. Fellows dropped to his knees and pressed his palms together as if praying. The psychologist put his palms on the floor and began turning his body in a circle, woofing like a dog. As Fellows' twisted face wound slowly past the window, Lennie glimpsed the eyes of a man who had fallen into a hellhole, but a man who was elastic, stretching, clinging to the outer edge of the hole by his fingernails. Lennie sensed Fellows might yet be able to haul himself out.

Joe tapped Lennie's shoulder and flashed a thumbs-up.

Lennie pocketed the fisheye lens, pulled his stocking back down, and stepped up to the door. The flaming head towered beside him. Lennie rapped hard on the timber panel. Seconds passed. It didn't open. He thumped the door, creating booms like a kettle drum.

Fellows opened up, holding a TV remote control to his ear as if it was a phone. "Is that triple 0? I need an ambulance," he pleaded with the remote. His pupils were as big as coat buttons. His grey face glistened with sweat.

Lennie crooned, "I...am your lost soul!"

Fellows' eyes seemed to have trouble locating his soul. Joe thrust his burning face at Fellows as if he was going to head-butt him, pulling up just finger-widths from the doctor's nose. He bellowed, "I...AM DONNA'S FATHER!"

Fellows shrieked. The howls reminded Joe of a feral pig being savaged by wild dogs in the native forest at *The End of the World*. Fellows slammed the door.

Screaming and the sound of breaking glass erupted inside. Joe bunched an arm and lined up the door with his shoulder. But before he could plunge, it opened: Carol was wide-eyed as Bambi. TC nudged her out. She almost fell into Joe's arms. TC followed her down the steps.

"I know I cooked up a decent brew," TC said. "But he's seeing some powerful spirits inside that house."

Thumping came from the wall beside them, from inside the hidden room. A dog barked, followed by yelps and roars. It was hard to tell the cry of man from beast. *Pow! Ka-Pow!* There was no mistaking the gunshots.

"Faark," said Lennie, touching a hand to his left temple. Blood glistened on his gloved fingers. He staggered.

"There!" said Joe, pointing at a small hole in the side of the building.

A bullet had ripped through the inner plaster wall and burst out through the external fibre-cement cladding. Lennie was still standing at full height, dazed. Joe put a hand on Lennie's shoulder and pressed him to squat. Carol and TC followed the lead.

Joe turned to the mother and daughter. "Get in your car. Get the fuck out of here. Call Pauls. We'll catch up."

Joe grabbed TC by the shoulder. "Give me your undies. Quick!"

"What?" TC clutched his groin.

"Now!" Joe glowered.

TC shed the underwear and pegged his shirtfront closed with the fingers of one hand. His other hand tugged its hem down, part-covering his skinny buttocks. He and Carol ducked and shuffled along the driveway towards the Corolla that was parked on the front lawn.

Lennie dabbed his wound with his fingers. "Feels like I've been hit with an icepick." He began pulling his stocking off his face.

"Whoa," said Joe. "Let me."

Joe touched the hole in Lennie's stocking. Lennie flinched but let Joe explore his wound. The stocking was torn to the skin which was weeping blood.

"Brain damage?" asked Lennie.

"Hard to tell with you."

Joe rolled the stocking up Lennie's face to the eyebrows, leaving the fabric bunched over the wound and his skull like a beanie. Joe folded TC's white undies.

"They clean?" said Lennie, curling his nose.

"Rather drip your blood over a crime scene?"

Joe tucked the makeshift field dressing under the elasticised textile. "How you feeling?"

"Never been fitter."

Another wave of thumping and barking burst from inside the secret room. *Pow! Pow!*

Joe, worried the gunshots would arouse the neighbours, glanced towards the fence. No lights on next door. Hopefully, they weren't in.

"Let's pull the curtains on this clusterfuck," said Joe, moving towards Fellows' door.

Lennie made a stop sign with a hand. "Change your gloves, mate."

Joe pulled the spares from his pocket, tucked the bloodied pair in. Lennie pulled the pistol from his waist and slipped the safety off. Joe followed him inside. The Narnia movie danced on the TV.

Pow! Ka-thump! The building's walls shuddered. Silence.

They edged through the sitting room in sallow light and entered the double bedroom.

"Hey. Rosco!" Lennie called into the open wardrobe, holding the pistol in front of him with both hands. "You still breathing?"

No reply. From inside the wardrobe, white light radiated. They shuffled forward. Lennie poked his pistol through the final doorway and yelled: "Boo!"

They stepped into Fellows' lair.

"Gad-zooga!" gasped Lennie.

Fellows was pointing his bloodied bum cheeks at them, his arms dangling by his sides, his right hand clutching a shiny revolver. One buttock was torn to tendons and bone. The doctor was leaning into a wall and completely still.

"No wonder he's not talking?" said Joe, moving in for a closer inspection. "Must've knocked himself out."

Lennie joined Joe for the deeper examination: Fellows' head appeared to remain attached to his body, but most of it was plunged face-first into the gyprock-plaster wall. It appeared Fellows had charged the barrier like a human cannonball.

Lennie grimaced. "That's a serious expression of desperation to escape."

"There's your catcher's mitt," said Joe, noting that Fellows' shoulder blades had been stopped by vertical beams in the timber internal frame.

"Oregon," said Joe, identifying the type of wood from splinters. "Clearly tougher than bone."

Lennie pondered. "He might have got through if he had a better run-up. Momentum is a powerful thing. Imagine if he'd got into the street."

A tremendous amount of blood was dripping down the wall from Fellows' throat and pooling at his feet.

"Reckon he's dead?" said Lennie.

Joe looked at Fellows' chest for signs of movement. "Maybe he's good at holding his breath."

Joe turned to the motionless animal on the floor. "Shame about the dog. He looked like a beauty."

The Alsatian was on its side, blood weeping from bullet holes, one of which had torn through its head around the earholes. A chunk of glistening flesh lay on the carpet near its mouth.

"Wasn't happy with his boss," said Joe, who squatted beside the piece of flesh. "Bum?"

Lennie eyed it. "Mm. Too much gristle." He took a couple of steps towards Fellows, whereupon he examined the part of his throat that wasn't stuck inside the wall.

"Ah. There's your problem," Lennie said, being as careful as a TV detective not to touch the corpse or step in blood. "Rover here has ripped out some windpipe and a serious bit of juggie. I'm surprised Rosco had the electrics left in him to hit the wall like this."

The phone started ringing in Lennie's pocket.

Pauline said: "What's happened? Carol and TC are in a right state. They're waiting for us on the other side of town. They said you got shot."

"I'll live," said Lennie, touching his aching temple. "Fellows won't. I mean isn't. Living, I mean."

"Listen to me," she said. "You two are in shock, or your version of it. Get out of there now. Mop the evidence, but don't spring clean."

"Roger that." Lennie hung up.

"That mask," said Joe, pointing at the freckled leather creation sitting on the wall-side table. "The red spot between the eyes. Look familiar?"

"I see what you mean," said Lennie. "But we better skedaddle."

In the sitting room, they identified the wine glass Carol had used by the lipstick stains, and picked up TC's school tunic from the floor. Joe stood on a chair and pulled the micro-camera from the corner of the wall, following up with the bedroom cameras and the one in the kitchen.

Lennie went through Fellows' clothes that were piled on the kitchen floor. He found his *Bolt Electrical* business card in the jacket pocket and talked to the ghostly suit. "I don't think you'll have call for electrical repairs in your new place, Rosco."

Satisfied that the house looked like the occupants had only ever been a madman and his dog, they stepped outside and Joe pulled the door closed behind them. The porchlight blazed.

"Aaww," said Lennie as they faced the outer wall of the hidden room beside the driveway. Fellows stared at them, eyes open; it looked like he'd stuck his head through a carnival photo-hole, but stuffed up his aim. His nose had taken a nasty turn on the way through and his chin had caught the lip of the hole, giving him a buck-toothed look.

"Shall I?" said Joe.

"It's the right thing to do," said Lennie. "But give me a sec."

He looked into Fellows' eyes, tut-tutted, and said: "This is what happens when you choose the life of a pedo scumbag, Rosco."

Joe nodded solemnly and used the fingers of his gloved hand to draw Fellows' eyelids shut. Joe's nose itched; he lifted his shirt collar over his mouth and nose and sneezed into the DNA droplet catcher.

A lightning bolt flickered in the night sky above the distant ocean.

*

Lennie climbed into the Firefly's driver seat, started the engine, and motored sedately along the street, keeping the headlights off for the first block.

Joe, seated in the armchair, used a gauze pad dipped in a jar of Pauline's moisturiser to wipe away his face paint.

En route to their rendezvous with Carol and TC on the far side of town, they debriefed Pauline about what they'd witnessed.

"What about the bullet?" said Pauline. "Won't it have your blood on it?"

"Hopefully it landed on the moon. Or over the fence at least."

"And if they find it on the driveway?"

"I guess the coppers will be looking for an innocent bystander who got shot."

"And didn't report it?"

"Concussive amnesia?"

Pauline smiled wryly.

"Besides," said Lennie. "I have this." He lifted a hand off the steering wheel and pawed the Jack that was dangling on a bootlace from the rearview mirror.

Pauline shook her head and touched the Jack too.

"Hear that?" said Joe.

White lights flashed around the Firefly. Thunder grumbled.

"It's funny," said Pauline. "Whenever a summer storm breaks, I get a fizzy feeling in my legs."

Joe looked thoughtful. "One day soon, Pauls, doctors are going to work out how to rewire the human body, and you'll be galloping around like a greyhound."

Pauline chuckled.

"But with nicer teeth," Joe added.

Rain pummeled the roof of the van; water poured down the windows. The windscreen wipers flew into a frenzy.

Lennie leaned across, patted Pauline's shoulder, and showed her a thumbs-up.

She said, "A washed bullet tells no tales, hey?"

At the bushland park, as the rain subsided, all five huddled inside the Firefly.

Wet-haired TC, sitting on an armrest of the sofa seat wearing fresh underpants under his school shirt, plucked from his travel bag what the label suggested was a bottle of Sailor Gerry's brown rum. He first offered his companions one of the green lollies from his jar which he said could be washed down with the rum, but no-one accepted.

"You need to work on your timing," Lennie advised.

Despite TC's guarantee about the integrity of the unopened rum, Pauline insisted on carefully checking the seal on the cap. She explained that she wanted to be very sure the contents did not extend beyond fermented sugar cane. There was enough weirdness in her head already from today's events, and weirdness, which was second nature to some inside the Firefly, was the sort of thing that people like her could overdose on.

Lennie and Joe nodded appreciatively at her self-awareness and took on board the compliment that she had paid them about their excellent tolerance for the strange.

TC handed out paper cups and tipped in rum.

Lennie and Joe told their companions more about what they had witnessed in Fellows lair and described their touching farewell to the doctor in the driveway.

Joe's nose itched, but he pinched it and beat the urge to sneeze.

Pauline said, "Are you OK, love?"

"Think I was allergic to something in that house. Feeling better now, thanks."

Lennie said, "I told you, mate. You're allergic to evil."

Joe grinned and sipped his rum.

Pauline said, "There's something in that, Joe. The human mind and the human body connect in ways that we'll never understand."

When the rum cups were refilled, a point at which Lennie felt the van's collective nervous system was sufficiently relaxed, he stood beside the small microwave oven fixed on a shelf against the wall and opened the door.

"Phones," he said.

The crew handed over the handsets they'd been given for the Fellows operation. Lennie closed the microwave, set the dial to three minutes on high, and hit start.

While the oven hummed, burning the phones' brains and extinguishing their vital signs, Joe pulled a large calico sack from a pouch at the back of the driver's seat and held it open.

"Clothes and hair, please," he said.

Carol took off her wig, revealing short-chopped blond hair, and dropped the fake mousy-coloured weave in the sack. Then she peeled off her false eyelashes. When she stood and pulled her frock up over her head, Lennie, Joe and TC tried unsuccessfully not to look at her torso which was mottled with dark scars.

Pauline passed a T-shirt and draw-string trousers to Dianne Runyon – the ex-wife of Toby Runyon, judge's son, unemployed film and TV producer, wife beater, psychiatric out-patient, and one-time video production consultant to Dr Ross Fellows, PhD, recently deceased.

"TC," said Joe. "The Keith Bourbon, please."

"I was growing attached to it, Joe," he said, taking the wig off and lowering it sadly into the sack. He removed the school shirt, shoes, and socks and added them.

Joe had already thrown the school tunic in the now bulging bag. TC swapped standing places with Dianne so he could change into fresh clothes. Then it was Lennie's turn to remove his shadow-man outfit. He left in place the stocking beanie with the makeshift wound pad. Joe returned to civilian dress while standing in the dark on the grass outside the van with the sliding door open.

"Hear that?" said Lennie, cocking an ear as he put his foot into an elastic-sided boot. "We'd better move it. Slow and easy."

Emergency services sirens howled in the distance, rushing to a call-out.

"OK," said Lennie. "I'll take the Corolla with TC. He knows a nice spot near Blacktown railway station where we can drop it off. It'll be reborn by some enterprising teenagers. Then we'll catch the train home."

Joe said, "You might want to stop for a little bonfire on the way." He handed Lennie the fat sack of clothes.

"Look," Lennie said to his weary and blank-faced fellow travellers. "This didn't quite go as planned. But as Joe and I have learned, *Clean up Australia Days* have a knack of drifting off course. TC and I will see you back in the big smoke for a proper debrief."

TC rubbed his eyes with his fists. "We killed a man."

Lennie leaned over and ruffled TC's hair. "Are you kidding? He picked a fight with a dog and lost. That's the bottom line."

TC smiled.

Sitting on the drink cooler, Dianne sipped rum and looked up at Lennie, elbows on her knees.

"Fellows," she said. "It wasn't you and Joe who spooked him at the front door, not really. After he got naked, before you came, he banged a broom handle on the ceiling raving about someone upstairs in a cling-film dress dancing, keeping him awake at night. Then he started yelling "you Munchausen bitch" into the fridge freezer. He pulled out a bone and started talking to it. I'm a nurse. I don't think it belonged to an animal."

Joe shook his head. "That mask. Fellows' mask. The red spot."

Gears clicked inside Lennie's skull. "The third eye."

"The third what?" said Pauline.

Lennie said, "Fellows had a leather mask in his secret room. There were freckles all over it. And a red spot between the eyes."

"Oh, my God," said Pauline, gulping as if she might vomit. "She was obsessed with the idea of the inner eye. That's why she got the tattoo there."

Joe lifted his rum cup. "To Miss Munch," he said.

"Miss Munch," his companions chorused.

"I knew I could smell a rat in there," said Lennie.

No-one smiled except Joe, who was thinking you had to have been there to get it.

Pauline dabbed a tear. "The police can surely put the puzzle together now."

Lennie patted her shoulder. "I think Rosco will be exercising his right to remain silent tonight. But that studio of his, and his freezer, will be saying plenty. I reckon he's gonna make the news."

24 - THE INNER CHILD

WHISTLING ALONG the Hume Highway in the little Corolla, TC snapped the top on a can of beer from a six-pack he'd just purchased from a booze shop next to a late-night pharmacy.

"Just the one, Lennie," said TC. "Especially on top of those pain killers."

Lennie held out a hand. "Are you my mother now?"

"Brothers, aren't we?"

Lennie smiled, sipped the beer, and tucked the can between his knees. He glanced in the rearview mirror at a wide, white bandage that TC had wrapped around his skull after disinfecting the wound at a roadside rest stop. A scarlet stain had penetrated the bandage. A thin line of blood trickled from under the dressing, sliding by the outer edge of Lennie's left eye, glistening on his cheek.

"You look like you've been in a war," said TC. "Like you're crying tears of blood."

"Don't get all poetic on me, for fuck's sake," said Lennie, whose bandage made him think of Rawcus. On the upside, they'd have something new in common to yak about when they got home.

TC sipped a cola and said: "That gardening project in the shed at *The End of the World*. Want to re-boot it?"

"Run your theory past me again? This whack on the scone is giving me short-term memory loss."

"Well, there's that native plant called *erythroxylum*. It's growing wild in the bush all around *The End* as you know, but no-one knows how to farm it. Not at scale. Now, if you match it with this plant from Easter Island called *schoenoplectus californicus*, or Totora in laymen's speak, we can create a super-compound that stimulates the body to produce molecules called *nicotinamide adenine dinucleotide*.

"Fucking English, mate."

"Let's call this *nicotinamide adenine dinucleotide*, NAD for short. Yes?"

"Good. NAD."

"NAD is the fountain of youth, Lennie. In the lab, I've worked with mice who were the human equivalent of sixty years of age. We fed them NAD, and a week later it's like they're twenty. We could make a fortune if we get it right and can take it to commercial scale."

Lennie looked at elfin-faced TC. Twenty-seven years of age, and he's getting away with posing as a twelve-year-old kid? Come on, Lennie told himself, wakey, wakey! TC was tucking into NAD, nothing surer.

"Do you have any of this stuff on you? Like a sampler?" Lennie said.

TC pinched the pad of an index finger against a thumb-pad and pretended he was curling the ends of a very mischievous moustache.

Lennie pulled his regular phone from his pocket and speed-dialled Joe on open speaker. Joe answered.

Lennie said, "Is that *The Owl and the Pussy Cat* I can hear?"

"You jealous?" said Joe. "Pauls just bought me *The Little Pig Robinson* audiobook as a prezzie when we fuelled up."

"Lucky you," said Lennie, who loved that story. "Anyway, if you can pull yourself away from little pig Robbie for a moment, I have a question."

The audiobook faded. "Shoot," said Joe.

"Do you want to get this *Fountain of Youth* thing back on track?"

Joe chuckled. "Why not?" he said. "What else can go wrong at *The End*?"

The phone connection dropped out.

Lennie had to love the big guy. Whatever else he was learning in adult literacy classes, he was now mastering irony.

Lennie scratched the drying blood on his cheek; the action opened a door in one of the dark regions inside his skull. Through it stepped a problem that was related to FOY: Lennie was pretty sure he didn't want to live in a world full of rich people who never died, and in fact got younger. Mm...they'd be the ones who'd get their grips onto high-quality NAD and hog it, nothing surer. Mm...the *F for Ethics Colour Scheme* – maybe that's how we could allocate NAD. And if we don't get onto it, sure as hell some other pricks will, people like all the other Fellows and Fellowettes in the world. But then, of course, young people, even rich ones, take more risks than old ones, die more often from accidents and misadventures. NAD won't stop that. So things might balance themselves out. Lennie's head started hurting from the ruminating.

"Fucking science," he growled. "It'd be alright if it didn't get mixed up with greed."

"What are you on about, bro?" said TC, who plucked a vial from the pocket of his chinos. He shook out a pill and washed it down with his cola. "Want one?"

"What are they?" said Lennie, sipping his beer.

TC did a pretend moustache curl. "Vitamin C."

"I don't have a pill testing kit."

"Trust, bro. You should try it sometime."

Lennie decided to consult the Norse God of Dawn, Delling, on NAD, but that would require a visit to the sea, aboard the *Flamingo Sky* with Joe and Rawcus, to watch the old master's brushwork on the sunrise. Something red then blue glinted in his rearview mirror. Uh-oh!

Police cars were approaching at speed, flashing lights, sirens blaring. The Corolla was already rattling at its maximum rate of knots that barely reached the speed limit.

TC glanced in the wing mirror and put his head in his hands. "God. How many years will we get?"

"Pop that hat on my head will you, mate?" Lennie replied. "And do your seatbelt up. I could lose my licence."

TC picked up an oversized straw sun hat that he'd purchased from the pharmacy along with the bandage. He put it gently on Lennie's head.

Lennie glanced at himself in the rearview mirror: he saw an A-grade bogan wearing a cheap hat in a shit-box car. He plucked the beer can from between his legs and tucked it into his door's side pocket. The red and blue lights settled alongside him. The beam of a spotlight shot down from the police car into the side of Lennie's face.

He glanced up into the light and smiled politely, holding up a hand to shield his eyes from the beam. He turned his gaze to the road. The police light probed the back seat of the Corolla. It returned its eye to Lennie's profile.

"We're doomed," TC mewled.

"Calm your pulse," said Lennie.

The spotlight went off. The patrol car accelerated and barrelled away, chased by a second patrol car, both vehicles pursuing something out of sight around a bend.

"Shit," said TC, who unclipped his safety belt and slid forward to the edge of his seat so he could get a better view out of the windscreen. "Do you think they're chasing Joe?"

"Dial him," said Lennie.

TC tapped the phone screen. "Still no signal."

Lennie put fingers into a jeans pocket to touch a Jack. He glanced in the rearview. White diamonds were expanding in the reflective glass. The pursuing vehicle flashed its headlights – once, twice, thrice.

Joe tucked the Firefly behind the Corolla in the outside cruising lane. Trucks and cars rushed past, the world in a hurry, always in a hurry. Lennie opened his window and stuck a hand out to send Joe a thumbs-up.

"What a day," Lennie puffed, expelling air like he'd just surfaced from a long, deep underwater dive. "Let's go home…"

TC turned on the car radio. "Is classical OK?"

Lennie nodded. TC fiddled with the dial. The speakers emitted a tinny sound; a stirring orchestral tune tried to assert itself inside the cabin.

"Ah," said Lennie. "A bit of *Apocalypse Now.*"

"It's from a German opera, Lennie."

"I prefer the film."

"*Ride of the Valkyries* was composed by Richard Wagner a hundred years before the film. But I can understand why you like it."

"So you're my psychiatrist now, as well as a music historian with the middle name Pompous?"

"Did you know the Valkyries were female messengers of the Norse God Odin? They rode into battle on flying horses. Your friend Delling was likely acquainted with them…"

Lennie tut-tutted. "You're speaking about them in the past tense, TC, as if they no longer exist."

TC rolled his eyes. Lennie smiled. Wagner faded. The fanfare for the radio station news bulletin chimed in.

TC screwed up his face. "Do you think we're subject matter?"

"News travels fast, but not that fast, I hope."

Lennie and TC cocked their ears. A potpourri of the day's political and business news crackled from the dashboard audio mesh…their ears pricked up.

An anti-terrorism taskforce has redirected a manhunt for twin brothers who are the target of a nationwide alert.

Christian and John Enoka, Australian citizens who were born in Samoa, are wanted on charges of financing and supplying arms to both Islamic extremists and white neo-Nazi groups in Australia and overseas.

In a bizarre twist in the case, the crew of a commercial fishing boat reported seeing the brothers alight from a cabin cruiser and board a merchant ship bearing a Panamanian flag in international waters to the east of the Great Barrier Reef early yesterday morning.

The fisherman said they recognised the brothers from their wanted posters.

The brothers are described as being two metres tall and morbidly obese.

The ship fired warning shots at the fishermen from a bow-mounted cannon before hoisting the cabin cruiser onto its deck by crane and heading deeper into international waters...

TC looked at Lennie. "I thought you said they were now as *skinny as rope?*"

"Maybe they've binged on Hungry Jack's since then. But that news story is probably A-grade bullshit."

"How so?"

"Theory one: the Enoka's paid or threatened the fishermen to spin the yarn to the plods. Result: it diverts law enforcement resources away from their arses, fat or skinny."

TC rolled his hands. "*Theory one* suggests that you have *theory two*, and possibly more."

"Theory two: the authorities know, or they suspect, the fishermen's story is bullshit. But they want Johnny and Chris to think the heat's off."

"So they plan to catch them nodding off, is that what you mean?"

"Pretty much. You've heard of the saying, *Follow the Fishermen?*"

"No."

"Nor have I. But if I was a plod, I would."

"I've been thinking," said TC, licking his dry lips. "Maybe I should move in with you and Joe for a while, just to be on the safe side. I can pay rent."

Lennie nodded. "We might have a room."

"Just don't make me sleep in that hole under your shed."

*

"You know," said TC, "there's something I don't understand about you and Joe."

"Pray tell."

"You guys love electricity, right? I mean, you run a business with it. And you're always carrying on about lightning and thunder. And you, Lennie, with your stars and your gods. Then Joe's in love with Mother Nature, thinks he's a whale in a human body."

"Your point?"

"Your Firefly Electrics van."

"I haven't got all night. Blacktown's the next exit." Lennie drained a beer and tucked the empty can into the pocket of the Corolla's door.

"You've got solar panels on your roof at home, but your key mode of transport is a van with a filthy diesel engine spewing carbon dioxide and other poison into the atmosphere. Don't you think it's time to change?"

Lennie flipped the straw hat off his aching skull and patted the pain. "Do you really exist, TC? Or are you my conscience turned into human form, this weird little child who won't shut up?"

"I told you not to drink on top of those pills, Lennie."

25 - IN THE COSMOS

AT HOME in the morning, Lennie sat alone at the kitchen table. He forked the golden yolk of a boiled egg into his mouth and rifled through his dead granny's metal hatbox. It was stuffed with faded photos, postcards, and pressed flowers. He extracted a dog-eared card sent long ago from the far side of the world.

In the adjoining sitting room, Joe plonked on the sofa fingering a TV remote. Rawcus and TC perched on either side of him. Joe surfed channels. On the big screen, terrifyingly well-coifed men and women, sitting behind desks or in armchairs, came and went.

"Any news?" called Lennie, who wondered how long the coppers could keep the lid on a story about a dead dog and a naked police force psychologist.

"Crickets," said Joe.

"Well, listen to this," said Lennie, reading from the old Norway-stamped postcard.

"What strange marvel did I see without,
in front of Delling's door;
its head turning to Hell downward,
but its feet ever seek the sun?"

"What are you on about?" Joe called.

"It's a Norse riddle! About our sunrise painter, Delling. Can you guess the answer?"

Joe pondered. "Is it some drongo who dove headfirst into a sandhill, so his feet are sticking up?"

"Not far off. I'll give you a hint. It's a veggie, mate."

"Vegemite?" asked TC, cocking an ear at the doorway into the kitchen.

"Crikey Moses!" said Lennie. "I meant vegetable, not the stuff you put on your toast."

"Hang on!" called Joe. "I think we're on."

Lennie bounced off the kitchen chair and bounded into the sitting room. He stood beside the sofa with his eyes on the TV watching pictures of a forensics team in hooded overalls carrying boxes from a suburban house that was fenced with crime-scene tape.

A young female detective wearing a business suit and open-neck shirt stood with a reporter on the lawn in front of the house.

Reporter: "So you found a dead man inside?"

Detective: "I can confirm the discovery of a deceased man, yes."

Reporter: "Can you name him?"

Detective: "We are contacting his family first."

Reporter: "How did he die?"

Detective: "It appears he was killed by a dog."

Reporter: "Where is the dog?"

Detective: "Dead."

Reporter: "Do you think third parties were involved?"

Detective: "No. It appears to be a tragic case of misadventure."

The reporter did a show-pony sign-off and the pictures returned to the TV station's horse-toothed news anchor in Sydney.

"Well," Lennie said to his companions. "We've jumped the first hurdle OK, by the sound of it."

TC squinted. "Do you believe what the detective said, about accepting it was a straightforward death by misadventure?"

"I don't believe anything I see on the TV," said Lennie. "But it'll do us for now. In fact, I wouldn't be surprised if they try and sweep Fellows and his evil shit under the carpet. How he died won't matter much when they sift his secret life. They'll be glad to have him gone."

Joe nodded. "Gotcha. Dead men tell no tales. What was that film? Pirates of the Caribbean five?"

TC tapped his phone screen and scrolled. "I think you'll find the expression dates back to a man named Thomas Becon in the year 1560..."

Rawcus rolled his eyes. "Shut up! You fool!"

TC looked wounded. Joe patted his shoulder.

Lennie waved his old postcard. "Let's get back to this riddle."

"We give up," said Joe, who found a sports channel and picked a tennis match.

"It's a leek!" said Lennie. "Its head is stuck in the ground, but its leaves fork up like legs and its feet grow towards the sun."

Rawcus climbed off the sofa cushion onto the armrest and hopped up to Joe's shoulder. He whirled his head in circles. "I'm seeing stars," he squawked.

TC grinned. He nodded at the front panel of Joe's ochre-brown T-shirt which was printed in chalky white lines with a grasshopper-shaped figure.

"Speaking of heavenly constellations, Joe," TC said. "That's Namarrgon from the Aboriginal Dreamtime on your shirt, isn't it?"

"Yep."

"I've read that he talks with thunder and wears stone axes on his head, and elbows and feet, so he can split clouds and make lightning that he throws at people who annoy him. Yes?"

Joe nodded. "I reckon he's got you in his sights."

"I never go outside in storms," said TC, whose expression brightened. "Did you know that the Hindus have millions of Gods floating in space? In fact, there are more than ten thousand separate religions worldwide and infinite Gods, some hanging around from Ancient Greece and Rome, if you go in for that sort of thing."

Joe looked away from the tennis, enthusing at TC's topic. "Don't forget Jesus and his dad, and that nasty prick, Satan."

Lennie stroked his chin. "What's that line from *Spinal Tap*? When they're standing at Elvis's grave, talking about the experience putting perspective on life?"

Joe nodded. "*Too much, there's too much fucking perspective.*"

Rawcus shook his head. "Blaardy hell. Life's a mystery, mate."

Joe smiled. Rawcus had nailed the routine rant of a wrinkled, front-bar philosopher at the Rose & Thistle. But Joe knew there was more than simple memory at work in the deep space of that feathered noggin, space that was far beyond Joe's grasp.

He winked at his plumed friend. "You're spot on, cobber. Spot on."

Rawcus nuzzled the big man's cheek. Lennie reached down and ruffled the bird's brilliant sulphur crest. TC caught the moment in a picture with his phone.

The End...for now.

Thanks for reading *Galaxy Motel*, Book #3 in the *Firefly Electrics Series*

Lennie, Joe, and Rawcus will return soon in Book #4, *Gumleaf Mafia.*

In Gumleaf Mafia, *the team sails from Australia aboard their yacht Flamingo Sky, heading via Tahiti for the fabled Galapagos Islands where they hope to drink a few beers and learn more about the evolution of life on earth. Too bad they are 200 years behind HMS Beagle and Charles Darwin, who didn't have to deal with rampaging tourists and resort hotels.*

They are also escaping the fallout from an investigation into mysterious happenings between a naked police force psychologist and a dog in a beach house near Sydney.

En route to the Galapagos, their old enemies, the giant Enoka brothers from Samoa, pick up their scent. Will the Enoka's foul-up the plans of Lennie, Joe, and Rawcus to sail on to Los Angeles on a mission to infiltrate the 'Gumleaf Mafia' of Aussie movie talent in Hollywood and rescue teenage twins who disappeared after an audition? Might the LA porn industry be in for a shake-up no-one saw coming?

***

Learn more about the Firefly Electrics stories at: www.markfurnesswriter.com

Other Firefly books:

In *Justice Machine*, Book #1:

Lennie and Joe thank their lucky stars when they are fishing at dawn on a city wharf and a small fortune falls from the sky into their laps during a cargo-loading accident. They escape without being ID'd, and know exactly how to distribute the windfall. But have their stars been knocked out of alignment?

When Lennie's ex-parole officer, Trixi Talaveda, drops into their home for a chat about the missing cash, accompanied by the giant Enoka brothers, life becomes trickier than ever.

Will this new peril derail their plans to re-educate a man who persuaded Lennie's beloved Aunty Doreen that money really did "grow on trees" - and drove her to the grave?

Might a sea voyage with Aunty D's tormentor aboard their little yacht, Flamingo Sky, solve all their problems? Or might it all end in disaster?

***

In *Kangaroo Court*, Book #2:

Lennie, Joe, and Rawcus are touring inside a mountain forest when they discover an abandoned campervan – and a pair of stringless tennis racquets. Who would own such objects, and why?

The deeper into the forest they venture, the more mysterious things they find. They're soon headlong on a mission to save strangers from a terrifying ordeal among the trees.

Meanwhile, their partner in a secret botanical business is abducted, forcing Lennie and Joe to confront demons from their past. Can they save the childlike young man they call The Chemist?

If that's not enough to juggle, their friend Pauline Gerrity rings an alarm from her refuge for abused women and children. Her call leads Lennie and Joe to create a sculpture they title Cocoon of Man and hang anonymously from an inner-city tree. An art critic likens their work to the British street artist, Banksy. But when the critic calls the tree-hangers "borderline psychos", Lennie and Joe aren't sure whether to be flattered or insulted...

***

Other books by Mark Furness:

Under Eden, an international crime thriller trilogy: *The Ebola Conspiracy; Freefall; Red Box.*

Short stories:

The Trespasser: Life of a Peeping Tom in 2021.

Drink with a Stranger: Journey to the Bizarre in Delhi, India.

Hugo's Awakening: A Mind-bending Road Trip to the Australian Outback.